THE FRONT MATTER,
DEAD SOULS

Wesleyan Poetry

Leslie Scalapino

THE FRONT MATTER

DEAD SOULS

WESLEYAN UNIVERSITY PRESS

Published by University Press of New England

Hanover and London

WESLEYAN UNIVERSITY PRESS

Published by University Press of New England

Hanover, NH 03755

© 1996 by Leslie Scalapino

All rights reserved

Printed in the United States of America

5 4 3 2 1

CIP data appear at the end of the book

The publisher gratefully acknowledges support of
Lannan Foundation in the publication of this book.

The author gratefully acknowledges the following journals,
which have published fragments of this work: *Chain,
Avec, Phoebe, Volt, River City,* and *Prosodia.*
Passages from this work have also been published
previously in Leslie Scalapino, *Objects in the Terrifying Tense /
Longing from Taking Place* (Roof Books, 1995), and
Selected Writings (Talisman, 1996); in *The Gertrude Stein
Awards in Innovative Poetry;* and by Meow Press.

Cover collage by Leslie Scalapino. The author wishes
to thank Hiraki Ukiyo-e Foundation in Yokohama, Japan,
and Mr. K. Kurashima for a photo of Tsukioka Yoshitoshi's
print, "Gojō Bridge, an Episode from the Life of
Yoshitsune (Gikeiki gojōbashi no zu)."

FOR TOM

THE FRONT MATTER,
DEAD SOULS

Introduction

The Front Matter, Dead Souls *is a serial novel for publication in the newspaper. Its paragraph-length chapters can also be published singly on billboards or outdoors as murals. Parts of it were submitted to various newspapers during the election campaign, though not accepted.*

A sentence might be such a chapter, such as "Hole of sumo floating on wave is not it."

The writing is to be as close as possible to nature itself not actually occurring.

I'm trying to write the modern world, which requires rewriting it.

A dialogue about love is utterly crucial to the remaking of the modern world in writing.

There can't be 'tradition of one's faculties' even.

This is a plot in continual series of actions. The writing of events is not a representation of these events; actions are not submitted to being made peaceful by doctrine or interpretation, that is, in a fake manner, but artificially *by finding their own movement and a dual balance in an impermanence of the structure.*

The form is to bring (actually to be) 'the American grain'

*or contemplation to an actual 'light life'—rather than 'myth,'
as this is 'structure' per se defining 'one' and phenomena.*

*This writing is scrutiny of our and 'one's' image-making,
to produce extreme and vivid images in order for them to be real.
It's as if an 'addition' to the Surrealists, as if also in reverse
'beauty as completely realistic.'*

Traveling is also the live world. Existing solely.

*Where the black butterfly not being seen in the blue air—
is one dreamed, is the action of events—that is life, not
dreamed—, that is only present.*

*Continual traveling, arising from the sense of the self not
being enough, or being nothing, brings the other culture to be
inner. It is one however not regarded by 'others' as and in fact
not belonging to one.*

THE FRONT MATTER

At the moment the wrestler is thrown sagging draped on the
mat.

A man squats in the center of a stand on a platform. His
clothes open showing his chest. He shoves flat fish on a long
wooden paddle.

One eats the salty sweet fish in the black night.

The serial in the newspaper is the same as lip reading.

A hyena is swimming amidst the lilies.

Distinguishing from floating in front of the lasso.

That barely comes up. The hyena gets the infant in its
mouth and swims with it.

It's swimming between the lilies on the lake with it. That
could be for something to drink.

This was pleasure for the new person in the city. The novel is dead. I make no distinction between being dead and being alive. It is dead as it is solely, so this is serial.

Then, it's inner; or outer, somewhere on the wave that ripples from or amidst a mass of people.

To have a play in which people speak what they don't say to each other is wondering what speech is? They may lip read themselves. But do that in this.

Eileen Myles still,
no image

in campaigning to be president when she is a poet there is our country's absent marginalia.

Then the black butterfly flying in the blue can't be seen in the blue.

The various cultures in disintegrating together, one can't see it in oneself. It's only occurring in the wave.

Perhaps the interior is qualitatively different from the serial.

Then how does the serial change? What is speech when it is not inner?

If we make this so simple it will not be what's public.

The figure is howling jealously from being born and bites any standing near still living. The rim's paired from one being born passing so close ill to those who're here longer.

A sound continues from the crowd as an immense bulk of sumo wrestler flops and is pressed. Holding the belt on the expanse of sash as the heavy haunches ram.

Anyway the infant is born blind and needing drugs which she's never had.

The sumo coming forward slapping with his palms, who's

resting on his crouched scuttling vast legs, has nothing inside; action is the core.

The rose dog brightly lit and enflamed, and at the same time with my anger occurring, didn't produce that. When someone had died, to that. Then the dog a sack, I released fury gutted inside lying unable to sleep—is in the crowd.

A hyena drifts by in front of the sun, in a business suit.

The blind moving their limbs are in the purple night as it dilates.

So there's not a difference between the ad and the time that's been eliminated.

It becomes immense and the blind people are washing in it.

There can't be speaking in it. The hyena in the business suit passing in front of the sun isn't seen by them.

Eating the sweet salty fish extended on the paddle by the kneeling man on the platform, there are no accumulated characteristics. If we'd stayed up until dawn we could have seen night still.

There's no one floating on the heavy green wave.

On the night, people who work for companies live outside.

As she lives outside alone, in that she doesn't have a company, she doesn't have any other attachment.

A squatting sumo runs slapping.

The night's hanging in the light blue.

Needing a job, however, Defoe enters the labyrinth of rooms behind the wrestling ring.

She goes into the room and Dead Souls is there being massaged, somehow spread like a clam.

With her mouth open, the latter's teeth have now been stained black. A white face in which the black teeth open faintly in red rim has brows that are black painted clouds over the shaven ones.

The latter gestures to Defoe without recognition.

The soft small bulk is wrapped in bathrobes.

I'm going against the very possibility of this.

I'm taking the outer now current culture *to be* the inner self drawing it in as one's core or manifestation—which it isn't. Then, it is externalized as oneself and is projected outward again as one's sense of real. That actually *is* one's inner self by acting upon its projection.

It is the specific instance of its action that is seen.

A patrician has a reflection of self.

Taking its actions into and as one is the point of madness.

We don't know having an inner mind so create it in it.

There is no ability. A crowd on the street hating, crying for infants to be forced to be born, an ill figure runs through the crowd.

Shots ring out, of a figure one time as one passes being torn up by the bullets from being in the crowd and biting some. It ran out through the crowd and bites any standing still living who're near. The crowd sweeps by.

The moon bulb's in a stream by them.

Wandering amidst the crowd, Defoe sees immense men. They are sumo wrestlers wearing loin clothes. Immense bulk, they have heads on them of thugs or handsome boys.

Defoe doesn't know she is sauntering, the limbs flowing. She has to have new work each time she works so as to not know what she's doing.

This is imagined as the utmost rigor, as having not to have formed anything, not to in the future. Yet to not form, or oneself to not be formed, can't be rigorous even, if it is to occur.

To be 'dislocated' never remaining as the same person by continual disruption is the creation of that 'one.'

A maroon dog nothing in itself emanates the bouncing rose on the sky as the bulb of sun wavers above half in it. The speck of the dog black floats there. It doesn't float there black.

The being of 'one' is conflict. She sees the real as only the present.

Dead Souls in love:
The part trembles when it is up in her. It floats above her with a handsome boy's head.

The head floating over her, he puts the long part in.
The vast haunches and belly squatting bent over her, puts the long extended part gently up in her.
His head swims over her.

The vast silken bulk held one time, wavering puts the part in her.
Swimming on her.

His immense haunches puts the part in, one time.
The wavering bulk moves coming. Then he leaves.

One time, he's straining with his part up in her comes.
His face floats in front of her then.

In the matted hair. The handsome head of the boy lips parted eats the red salmon roe.

One time she's on him who's motionless. He comes then.
Sail on the frogs in the black air. Sailing eating them.
Defoe goes by some swinging doors to a room one time.
She sees a woman entwined with the immense bulk on which is the head of the thug.

His eyes are half-closed with the vast hard gelatin frame moving slightly as his part is in her.

His eyes close and open slightly as he withdraws his long part from her.

She's spread trembling. There's a space. He sticks it and the vast haunches moving comes, with his eyes floating over her closed.

The woman comes then just after, inner.

Events here become the inside of *this*, by being its fiction. The Oakland hills ablaze

The sumo wrestlers are running out. An immense limb flaps softly in the vast air.

We watch someone beaten rolling on the video. Then the jury says he was in control, when he's being beaten there.

The first thought was they should beat the jury, that would be just. That is without knowledge of government.

Knowledge of government takes a lot of preparation before.

So forget it.

I'm trying to get the real event. It's a balance as to when the real event emerges.

The sumo wrestler's eyes are tiny fish lost in the mass that's floating head on it.

The woman's folded with her legs up on her.

He puts his member in her.

They can't be seen. Eating the frogs by sailing in the blackness. They're living on the blackness.

Hovering over her, he draws it out. It's night.

Defoe comes to the latter's door, who comes out the clam's robes still open disheveled. The blackened teeth around which her mouth smiles slightly are seen in the shadow.

The member of the vast bulk of the sumo wrestler with the handsome head of the boy withdraws from being in her.

She hastily puts her bathrobe around her.

From behind her, the part standing up is seen on the immense hard gelatin without his loin cloth at the moment.

There's a faint rim of white powder on the other woman's lips, who says in a low voice directed back to him to take some package to her van.

Then she shuts the door on Defoe.

A man ran in the crowd biting some.

One saw him roaming; blood only appeared on people in the crowd.

A woman dragged a cord behind her through the crowd where people ran.

One time, Defoe comes to the pond outside. A roiling mass of carp emerge out of the surface, a hard head of one touching her hand as it protrudes splashing from the water.

In the water bulk the handsome head of the boy the black hair pinned on the vast surging trunk rises, swims in the ocean like a walrus.

Defoe turns around from looking at the ocean. Passing the pond, she goes to the latter's (Dead Souls') door.

who's open spread as a clam but away from her. She can't see what's inside the folds of robes, which the boy has just left.

Suited men are outside on the street leaning on cars. One time, a man dark-haired spikes finds her and begins questioning her. His eyes almost closed and his lips parted, the women employees run in little steps even when there's no one apparently watching.

They simper seeming to bow even when they're running in the little steps.

His eyes are steely when he opens them on her. He asks whether she knows her employer is a dealer, and regardless she's an accessory unless she's willing to inform for him.

His black hair jagged is shaved around the base. The pear-shaped eyes open. He's stopped her outside under a tree.

Defoe says nothing.

One time, he tells her to wait. She's in her employer's office, and he who's there now continually seemingly working with or for the latter, again asks her to inform.

Sullenly, she fiddles with a music box on the latter's desk; a figure on it is of Minnie Mouse who jumps rope on a hop-scotch when the box is wound. Defoe can't say anything, confused.

There's a clear lane thinly men running.

This should have pictures with the writing meeting these at the sides so it is horizontal in blocks. That's utterly fabricated.

The columns of the newspaper have the pictures with the writing read down, yet read across, read slowly. She sees the gray featureless ratlike face of the man without a mouth as if it's stitched inward, on thin suited body running.

She looks back and falls.

The man without a mouth comes up beating her with his fists. He leans over her, beating her stomach and face, his mouthless almost eyeless gray pointed oval close.

Defoe has the illusion of the slender man (jagged-haired Akira who'd asked her to inform) waiting watching the red oval with his eyes down.

The rim is staring. He'd picked her up carrying her.

The rim the mouth sleeping itself. Which is Dead Souls floating in the light blue watching.

The cicadas are screeching in a din that rises and falls at one, filling the trees and grass.

The din sweeps and is the heat.

They're chattering at one above in sweeps.

A dog trots off from the walk. There's no blue.

The adult rejects the sense that the physical state will not end, that sense which was grasped in the light lucidity after the operation. Then the adult saw there's no death of one; none of us as utterly clear only in the physical state will die as it's endless.

The sand is a mere rim reduced vast above which is a chair where he'd sat drinking a scotch; Akira stooping with his hands on the railing of the balcony.

She's walking in the waves of the insects' din. A woman passing in the blue blistering rim is howling, jealousy driving her.

One bends forward into the bow of that blue.

A stream of dusk clings to it where a crowd is crying.

On the blue blazing, one could touch her in the bow to quiet her.

Getting back to the wrestling ring in Venice Beach, she sees it's silent.

The next day, waking, she sees the head bobbing on the immense bulk of the sumo wrestler in a wave.

The wave comes down softly with the great weight floating.

The half-closed eyes of the thug's head lie on the beach on the sagging carcass.

Defoe sees the latter bending by the immense carcass whose throat has been cut.

The news media grinding with cameras on the beach, the latter's folds are blowing, her blackened teeth visible with her mouth open slightly.

At night, Defoe comes to the latter's room. Who opens the door, her face blurred by drink, streaked. Blowzy, in the background the loin cloth on the immense hard gelatin who comes to the door behind her. His handsome head floats above.

The door closes.

The great weight slumped on the beach was under the moon. Motionless sagging out it is lapped by a few small waves.

The air becomes blue and hot in being thin.

The moon's in a stream, in which a figure's tormented with jealousy and bites one there still alive.

Bimbos that are men and women who are blond go out on their boards on the waves.

Their memory is expanded.

There's a memory of the half-closed eyes of the thug's head cut obscured on the massive bulk lying softly.

Read across, it floats. In the inky dark.

The crowd is in the train car, having been packed in by a man on the platform pressing them in through the door who uses his feet.

Behind the head of the pursuing rat-like figure suited surrounded by suits in the car.

It surges through the door in a wave. The black head turned away is amidst it; Akira appears to move in the lines of the crowd coming toward him. The gray without a mouth is held back in the car. Slash of twisted without mouth lunge behind the window of the moving train car.

The movement of the billboards in the tube with the tearing train has no terrain, islets opening. They flicker with the silk suit running in them. Neither memory nor the present occurs.

Emerald green swans rest in the water not having to move in it; a pool swims in the movement, an ad.

The heavy basins of the emerald green swans fly to her in the tumultous sky. There's no entity but there's action.

The howling figure on the train who'd beat her or appears to be him runs.

A platform clears. In the car, the gray stitched in head is darting. Men are reading bent over pulp comic books in which are text, one reading pictures of outer space creatures and men having dispute who then sometimes put their member, that of the creature or a man, in a woman who's lying with her legs back, then dispute continues. Gray silk suit on stitched head gets off at the next stop.

There're only one's events. One is not in them, and a memory occurs.

Trace that memory which is as if a streak. Or trace the events leading to others.

Rat man running through the cars, who'd missed the stop, has no other place.

Inducing happenstance, that has really occurred, is to bring it close together where one is a swimmer superimposed on it blind. It can't be seen.

Businessmen are beating a figure rolling in black robes who has a child clinging alongside.

The black waves on which the head of a sumo bobs aren't even seen. That's the utmost scrutiny existing.

L.A. not having a belief system is that, now our earlier innocence as we defined that in ourselves (which then isn't). It does not adhere to learning or see by custom. It can see by eyes. There are eyes floating in its horizon rim.

The children sipping gasoline, come up sniffing, are coerced to work for the drug dealers. In the interior everyone is coerced to work for them.

This is the main business in our country, really everywhere which is structured on it, the new world. A dug-out boat coming up at a 'town' where paste comes.

In the ring, the immense bulks grapple, their arms surrounding each other the enormous thighs shift slightly. Then one's flopped, the winner turning away floats. Eyes in the immense form turned down.

Handsome head squats balanced on his feet, the haunches bobbing on them flexing in the ring. Wipes his hands throwing the ceremonial salt.

The night's black riding.

The physical state has no end.

There was the roaring of a green wave on which the sumo floats.

No red rim on the neck as it is a huge hump lying on the thin surf is there.

The slender man jagged straight-haired in the loose suit is now lounging smoking out on the patio alone having a drink.

A small breeze ruffles his hair at the moment so that a spike of it stands forward over his forehead.

His legs relaxed. Wearing dark glasses sips a whiskey occasionally. The dark ocean is far off though the sand comes up to the walk across which he sits. A bicycle just goes by on the walk.

If there's not a difference between the ad and the time that's been eliminated, that's memory.

Blonds that are men and women in halters and g-strings start off over the sand with a dog.

There's woman carrying a board goes off on the sand with a dog.

She sees the man standing alone by a neon in the evening air.

The air's indigo then. With a g-string, his part is standing up in his middle and extended.

The long part is put in her and then withdrawn, when he has nothing on but the g-string. which slips off.

His arms trembling in muscles that are tense as he leans over her, the long part is up in her.

She moves on it. He sticks her, one time.

In the indigo air, he withdraws his part from her, with it bending downward extended. As he's on his elbows. She's folded with the part not in her.

Then he puts the part back in her. Outside.

She's curled, with the extended part not in her—hanging outside, from his middle. It shifts outside of her.

He puts it in her.

He comes. Then stands.

One time, they're inside, there's sky above the walk where a bicycle is passing.

He withdraws his part from her, then puts it in.

Lying flat on her, moves slightly flat coming.

The part is hard standing up in his middle when he is seated in a chair, one time.

The window's open blowing.

She lies down and slipping over her, he puts the stick in her up inside.

One time, Dead Souls calls to her. She gathers her robes and appears at the top of the stairs. He'd pulled his part out of her with it extended hanging standing behind her.

One time, she's eating the salty sweet fish with him with the heads bobbing around the stand outside.

Akira says the media here says ten-year-olds here are out of shape, can't run ten miles; you wouldn't want a ten-year-old to run it. The roar of the ocean and voices are muffled over the ring.

The roar and voices sweep.

The rungs that are tiers of the department stores are open with windows exposing people eating and drinking swept at tables on that tier.

One passing by looking up sees them. A soft thigh of a woman with crossed legs is at a glass table.

Billboards and neons flag, looming vast flags over the streaming cars.

How can we be the same as this only, tiers.

Afternoon people shop, yet the later it is the more evening

wear is seen on the people veering amidst the cars crossing below.
They make a separation.

One puts the white mud on one's face circling the eyes as others are lined up seated at the little tables with bibs on, for the demonstration in the department store. Walk through them.
Riding the escalator to higher rungs, gray silk suits brush by. The bone in the back balances itself. Were there playing pool it's a stick, in one. It straightens in the soft back.
Great bouquets for weddings spread massively.
On a bus, it itself is remembered, as if pictures of what had been in the bus swimming on themselves, while one is in it.
Everything's cracking the air's black and a dark red sun floating there's nothing. The pillars of the highway jutting beside are quiet.
The stick in the back swims.
Crowd of gray silk suits presses walking.

There is one who is abusive to others asking to abuse or if that's not accepted to reject them as something to do.
This is a streak as of memory. Maybe it is for attention to it.
Flattening that.
Giving that up, there's the flat plate of the ocean in front of which is the darkened mound of obscured half-closed eyes on immense darkness floating.
The sumo wrestler in the thin surf floats.

The lips say curtly to make her deliveries, such-and-such; closes the door on her. The rose Cheshire mouth hangs in the light blue afterwards.

A thick green wave begins, but in which thug-head sumo

rolls. She bends over on the sand, before the green wave, a thin cut on the vast sack, sagging in the shining trays of lit foam.

A black slender hand in the blue, the officer has her in his expanse as he walks flowing in a wide plain with the trays coming in even waves. As if she's bowing to the officer, her robe floats on her where kneeling she turns over the head that had rolled whose dulled beads reflect.

The sunlit trays of sea on which the huge sumo carcass, whose throat had been cut in a thin rim, floats on the water coming in has in it the employer's floating robe as she wades to his sack.

There's only an emotional landscape. That isn't even in the dead light wood figure that therefore floats.

But if one is deathless (in 'the deathless day' 'the physical body has no end'—as grasped in the light blissful lucidity that was after the operation) it is possible to see this landscape. One can see this living realm.

Walking under a glass dome, there are above it millions of black birds. They're flying and massing in a funnel in the sky. Scurrying in the dome the crowds of gray silk suits pass.

The bird in the furnace firestorm lies in the street falling beside one.

When the bird falls one thinks there's two minutes to get out of here. But later it opens.

When the red ball separated from the ink the long line of fire trucks came winding in stream of thousands of them on the pillars. The event appeared to be just then, separating from the ball on the black before the trucks came on the horizon and while there.

That instant of the line of cavalcade floating isn't produced by anything. I was soaked crouching on the ball.

The simplicity of the character collapsed as American in

the sense of having been nature. Being at that orifice at the real event occurred.

If I don't dream, which I do, there's no separation. So one has to see here.

The faceless stitched gray head is brushing in the bimbos that are men and women who are blond carrying boards floating with their legs in the air. She gets on the bus.

The rows in the bus are watching a T.V. mounted in front on which are sumo wrestlers, one cast aside as the other gently turns away swaying to return to the side.

Static interrupts as the next vast gelatin in the sash grapples without seeing in the air toward one much smaller. The rows in the bus release, static blurring it, frustrated. The faceless figure is riding in the bus with her.

The bus giving off the crack of its breaks when she's on the walk pulls away.

Behind, staggering gelatin motionless slightly quivers putting the feet down turning away.

So people become very old, shrunken and die, so what? in the future? Just omit.

Defoe is running after leaving the bus with the faceless figure behind her, the small gelatin soft thighs hurrying.

The crowd is crouching, releasing running. As the faceless silk suit is shooting. Rolling on skates. We've seen that. There's nothing that can be seen. So this flattens that, doesn't return to it.

Wind comes much stronger hot from the fire itself so it makes it up. Yet roiling on that street it came bearing down on one who is small.

Fire trucks are steaming in from the window, on the phone, there are cinders like cakes that spew, the washed bird. Black sky floating red ball after are the dregs.

The dregs running

Emerges onto the ring, calling crowd, the billows of clouds are in the air. Above.

The sumo floats sagging on the green wave. Rests on the thin tray of it, when the wave's not heavy.

It's heavy on which he floats and he's still floating on it when it's thin. Compare that.

A moon comes up when he's still vast bulk that's still on the sand.

Just seen between the rim of the wave. It curls.

She's short of breath, bursting into the office fumbling in the desk.

Emerging with a revolver, she's standing thin panting slumped on the wall.

Plastered on it panting and before her the vast dark shadow of sumo as of floating in thin surf holds the stick man in the air on immense silken slabs that rise to the handsome head of the boy.

Ask him what he wants, the panther plastering the wall panting says. Immense floating gelatin not seeing or listening carries the stick.

NEXT CHAPTER

The quiet imageless eyes float in the sockets.

Whatever Akira was waiting for isn't going to occur at all. That's the self being too stable, but he is not one, deliberately not a construction of oneself. He's on the occurrence ahead only in existence.

So he's separate from one, which enables event brought

to him and one not fictionalized. Yet even still it doesn't occur in nature.

In Mei-mei Berssenbrugge's *Sphericity*, the writing can 'see' "when a point is silent, not a vantage point."

Where everything changes, where there is no vantage point or sound in writing, "she couldn't say the experience or absence is changing"—nor is such existence *per se.*

The gray mouthless stitched face in the silk suit isn't tried, though arrested. He's later released simply, the red splice on rim of the sumo's neck on vast dark bulb being before in thin surf.

This is a serial to be in the newspaper. That's all. It has to really be done.

One's mind can't be suppressed. The moon racing in the desert is one resting.

The elation is clear and real, that the physical state is endless.

It's printed in installments, so some information is repeated. Sometimes it doesn't introduce anything. Only the fire storm arose from kindling.

Hole of sumo floating on wave is not it. Not wavering sags on the thin surf.

The contrary expectations are seen to be fabricated in the adult, one, who believes the elation is not realistic. One is swimming on the roof with the hose watering it in the inky air.

Soaked pouring crouching at the red ball. The sumo crouched huge on the thin surf a slab has the moon in it.

The moon hangs on the heavy green wave where the sumo's still, vast.

It doesn't create it nor is it in memory.

It's as close as possible to the condition of not actually occurring, while it is here.

next chapter   19

Because if it's my mind that's creating it, I can't get to the point where it will not have done that. I can't get it to occur.

Then sometime, cars began to come in cruising, filled with boys leaning out ogling.

The only police came later slowly cruising after the cruising cars packed with boys that went by. The hills were sheets of flames and dissolving frames.

Collapsing locations onto other places scrutinizes them. It doesn't now. Or juxtapose.

It's motionless in one. Objective is only its occurring.

On a bridge, so cars are driving on the jewel of a bay above it.

While Bechtel is reconstructing the oil fields ours have bombed, in the oil fields their foreign workers who're treated like slaves are executed for sympathizing with their invaders.

Their foreign workers can't survive in their own countries. They will then work for Bechtel.

That's a poem.

We work for Bechtel as writers who show the imperial world. So this is for my donor. The subject.

A hundred and seventy thousand infants maybe died there from starving or disease after the bombings.

A crowd here wearing yellow ribbons is crying for infants to be forced to be born.

One separates from them wearing yellow ribbons and running in the dusk.

The woman is in the blue stream floating on the dusk. In pain and jealousy she's able to be touched by someone in the bow. One leans on it bulb from them on the dusk.

Movement (or shape in writing) is a knowledge that isn't

one's thinking *per se*. One's thinking by itself is movement that is knowledge.

In a poem I wrote, *way*, I wanted compassion objectively *to be* in the moving shape there, as the form in the series— pressed in its moving of shape in the real events. It occurs not subject to one and outside of one.

I was trying to get a shape, which is in some way a sound, that's movement in location, and is also compassion by itself (objectively) occurring (*not* imposed) in these locations.

The writing is the minute moving or shape of a real event. Sentiment has no relation to existence. It isn't an act?

One is to be divided from one's natural mind as if that were inferior here.

That we are to conform *per se*, is what would not be ugly, be alone.

Where in the minute shape of a sole event one is there— but not in the entire series subject only to its own moving— *where* one is doesn't exist.

Here I resemble the real events *without* a recurring movement as their articulation in language. It's just out there.

Continual worry is barred by the elation in a light lucidity.

A worrying, that is born in external series of events endlessly, always recurring unrelated to one, is the sole inner suppressant.

The clear elation isn't keeping count in endless space, the light at dawn coming up over the city, being in that.

It is the worry itself that is death.

This was pleasures for the new person in the city. Only. Small businesses collapsing, shops featuring flimsy items are for survival.

People eating out are close to the sewer class.

Sometime, the long cavalcade of fire trucks came in

next chapter

thousands of them on the empty sailing pillars of the overpass. Sitting on the roof watching them wind slowly in, soaked crouching on it, see the blood red ball floated.

The small shop closes, one after another quickly. Someone or figures sitting in windows of restaurants eating are close. Their motion is having little, and so occurring.

I only have these thoughts. I can't seem to be someone else, though having the ideal that one should be.

But if one makes only these motions they're making motions there.

There's no relation between reading pornography and justice. The justices see nothing wrong with it for themselves.

His actions make him a distilled cretin. The distilled cretin as the justice bullying women is thereby appointed to the Supreme Court. Actions are reduced to base. Action is that, a base.

That is the point at which madness is produced. Not from oneself.

It isn't produced from dreaming.

Waiting for a dream to come up to observe the day. Not in it. Or compared to it. Nothing's reflected in either then.

One's still fighting inside in it. This produces swimming in one. Then, one dreams.

Korean man whose wife makes him smoke his cigar outside on his stoop puffing pleasurably sat in front of the fiery hills dissolving in flames from which chunks on fire sailed and landed burning.

The first lady disembowels women who are working in a line. They're to be at home according to 'their' ideology, but they have to work to live.

Caricatures are in the mind first. So that is most simple is involuntary in writing. Young life before the dinosaurs was multitudinously varied. We become more simple in structure with time.

Deep rose-jewel of glittering intestine lying embedded in the fetid corpse, the frame of which, lies on their ruin, the coiled gel in it appears to float.

This is current so its producing can't last.

One could go to where it had not formed.

The sumo where there's not the red rim on the neck on the immense carcass in surf, slowly rams in the ring.

Handsome head fallen:

His lips swoon themselves merging under the lacquered pinned hair as he's fallen in the ring on his back.

The vast bulk with the pinned hair flickering driving, the moon is above the people who come out walking on Rodeo Drive.

Going to a restaurant, the sumo the black hair pinned bobbing in front of the white orb stepping out of the car, goes in.

There're so many beers on one table, the platters are piled up. The vast mass spread squats. The latter, Dead Souls, who's an astute entrepreneur is being approached to get into dog racing, during dinner.

The round white orb is hanging later over a sand-colored straw field on which they stand as a greyhound runs in the dark and illuminated air.

Running so swiftly it can't be seen in the dark and appears out of it as if it were a bird its legs are folded on its body in the moonlit air.

The moon's bright and one can't see the legs even.

The characteristic of the serial novel is that it's published in the newspaper and so it's written chapter by chapter where there's no accumulation in that an event has to come up in it again.

Bravado is false action, fake. The ego being simply in the reverberation of its reaction, it's scrutiny. Therefore it's inner, not produced by one, because it's required.

next chapter   23

See it the first time.

Social perception doesn't function in writing. At all. It's inert.

Where the man lying in the street who's not successful is one's inner self is not sentiment.

Positions of erotica occur in this which are love then. In those exact minute motions; these have a rhythm of presentation in this that occurs in spurts and not planned. When it is subject to only its movement, it has no other reflection. It isn't social perception; or rather, is it *only* then. What's that?

They're out at a restaurant on Santa Monica Boulevard. There's a roar at the table, squat sumos with the black hair pinned and the small figures amidst them. The table swims with beer bottles and platters.

Driving in the convertible they're under the dark velvet air and the city light lying in it in which people are passing alongside.

Later the greyhound flies with its legs folded up on its body in the moonlit air for them.

The minute movement in the small shop ceases.

Patrician sentiment simply forms social class *per se*. For itself.

It can't last.

So the writing has to cross over the edge in space.

Silent reading is inner so it inverts in that it is centralized appearing to be pervasive, when the person is alone.

It has sunk retentive not appearing to be a motive. Therefore the figure working not accomplishing anything fills the shimmering sky turning a valve on the edge of a salt flat.

That's a motive. Still this so its motive isn't there.

We can't keep up with being resembled.

When Defoe comes to the latter's door with a message,

handsome head with the black hair pinned floats up behind the latter, his part standing up having taken it out of her.

There's a tapping and swaying of the lithe greyhound behind them as it crosses the room from inside. It's gentle doelike creature coming forward tapping that are folded up not visible on it in the air, when it runs.

The dogs at the track, for the latter takes hers out, waiting for it in the bleachers, are pins racing.

The latter, dressed up, in the parking lot the gentle creature taps swaying circling her is almost invisible when facing her.

It runs, a pin in the air.

Maybe memory itself is joy. It hasn't occurred, and that's it.

They're lurching in the subway holding straps as it shudders. Some reading, swaying as they hold the text open on a man or creature with his member up in a woman. The beginning of printing made the so-called mind first.

It occurs in the separation. Printing caused the separation.

I just want to observe writing on space.

If nature isn't occurring that's at the level of the gel chest floating in the dusk air.

This was to be written on billboards, that it never occurs. There's an opening to not occurring even.

It's not future in the sense of it's occurring. Action occurs before the newsprint and can only emerge at the level of (that is nature not occurring at) the line of the object in newsprint.

No object can be there.

They have to be born.

So things are by being in the dusk night here. A person is wandering beside it.

I was going to the movies. Men in the meter parking lot destitute quarrel over whose turf it is to wash the windows of the arriving cars. Coming back after, to one who walks up

next chapter   25

seeming out of it saying he's put money in the meter which has run out. The other man from earlier, who'd washed the windows, says he'd put the money in the meter. There isn't any in it. One could expect a reward. It's dark. There aren't many cars in the lot. He'd been waiting for hours.

Where one holds no assumption whatsoever, one can't have any past to have that even begging.

The minute movement in the small shop continues brought to where it's just stilled, where in time the movement is reduced without the small shop closing.

The small shop just closes maybe. Another opens.

He's on a burning ghat then. The burning ghats of L.A. enflamed brightly, a crowd stands crying. Dogs run on the outskirts of the field.

One should have no ability to do it there, which is inherent.

So movement is stilled.

Sumo with the handsome boy's head is lying on her resting on his arms, still and screwing. He delays. He comes.

He gets up with the part still and extended.

One time, she's standing and he's just taken his member out of her. He's standing behind her with the member extended up.

Which is seen when he's come to the door. Defoe's had a message for her. Then he puts it back in her.

Sleeps at night, the dog folded in the hall.

There's a park in the middle of the city that's a lotus pond with leaves of an enormous span, people walking over the bridge that crosses it.

The greyhound is visible from its side flashing around the latter, who's dressed up walking to her car. It's morning, the greyhound is invisible running out from her ahead. Then reappears with its legs folded up on its body sailing.

Can't be seen on the boardwalk.

Bimbos who are blond stand on boards here and there on the waves, an arm up with hair under it and on the chest is seen for a moment under the curl of a green wave. Then submerges.

Dog reemerges in the air toward her.

When there is no worry recurring not being sustained in the light elation

there isn't death; no days are sustained in it either.

The latter rises earlier seeing the light morning air. She goes down to the street where buses are giving off a clap of exhaust.

Still wearing her robe unfurled she's in the bright shallow light.

The black painted brows are smeared slightly on her forehead.

A tour bus for the wrestling ring is turning in on the street.

Heads emerging on it from it are going to be in the small shop. Minute movement there is objective at the moment.

The figures in black robes have children clinging to them and women who are in the army around them are not allowed to buy food without a man with them. Time isn't change.

The writer honors the ornate world. This is for my donor. Here they want to force the children to pray in the schools, to their deities who're them. Yet in believing anything it isn't it. One can have no goal.

Handsome boy's head with pinned top hair lacquered floats ahead in the night and figure that's invisible though occasionally seen with the legs folded up on it hurling goes back and forth around him.

Senators have smut for a mouth.

Looking in at someone shooting up in a green light, one doesn't exist. Standing looking down a block that's for people on crack, they're slumped in the street or wandering, who don't

next chapter

see one. A clear memory occurs of several people bending over here and there in the street, who're decimated and no longer existing then.

One has to be totally alert at all times.

The hair lifts on them from the violent breeze of the blades, the swimming green air murky. Sometimes during the day the helicopter sails over in the dense pea air.

Waves of white sand of dunes float on the desert.

The green air at night with her under it looking up, a flapping occurring coagulating in it forming is the president's helicopter. The blades cutting the green velvet air, go over in the path that is to his California ranch.

Green velvet air coagulating that surrounds it, that's silence where the copter wallows heavily over the figures in which the roar of the blades cutting is underneath.

There're neons and billboards lit that straddle the streets looming clogged in the arcades. That swims in the pea air, day and night. That existed as joy which isn't a memory.

The serial novel is conceived as it goes along.

Movement ceases in it, having any action as being action. The jewel begins forming in Defoe, to be born here. The blades cut above her in the heavy green air.

Events are completely ephemeral. That's what I want. They're fabricated as such. Just keep going. It doesn't create but this is doing so still.

A bulb tenuous on a muscle is floating on the garbage. Hanging over the garbage cans, from one to another, the bulbous empty muscle wavers at night.

He's gutted and so is at night.

He doesn't hallucinate on crack. Rather, night hallucinates him, as he's moving in it.

He's blind in that sense. Yet it moves with him as a muscle.

Night is without him, while he's there in it. He's a bloom as of the lotus in it.

The addicts move away in it. The night dilates so as to be. The place of 'reporting' is a mirror of night here.

As the blades cut a swath in the fume, there are troughs up to which the crowd has come.

Coming to the trough, the crowd is strewn like sheep as they're going to it.

Seen from above.

Crowds at the various troughs feed still.

Trash in this respect's without thought.

Since the media takes a brief time resembling them, continually, they exist without it now.

They're mirrored in it appearing to be dead. I want to produce that separation. It isn't thought.

Going over the people strewn appear.

Helicopters that are the police chase figures in the darkness. Lying in bed, one sees the round beam of their spotlight go by and return searching outside.

There's no poem, as the rod in the back is gel.

If memory is involuntary but continuous and repeats things that do not occur, it's mechanical as translucent.

Black night so therefore the orange sky occurs.

To say that the hole, oneself, is the same as events, doesn't see it.

The rod in the back doesn't make it. That's joy which hasn't occurred. It's still, evanescent.

This is to be as close as possible to nature itself not actually occurring. It is the blue bubble that's real which bursts (the other in oneself is fictionalizing).

This has to be on the bulb's strand because nature is. Which is because it's beautiful.

There's a dark rain and the figures washing in it are illuminated briefly by the beam from the heavy pan of helicopter churning when it is sagging on them.

next chapter

Why is there sleep for anything? What is that? The men are lying in ditches sleeping.

Therefore seeing it first can't occur.

They have to sleep or they'll die.

So they move like the minute movement in the small shop.

The tour bus arrives, turning in at the roar of the ocean and voices at the ring.

So it doesn't matter if one knew it before. Objective is its occurring at all.

The very purple oceanic wash has orange sky above it. When it was black, the darkened immense mass of sumo lies on the thin surf.

It's a plate. Then swimming.

The latter, inside with her handsome boy's head hanging over her opens the folds, the robes and puts his member up in it.

His immense mass is then black and therefore invisible as its dark.

It does exactly the market. She comes and he's resting in the black air, after.

One time, he's flat whose head is invisible turning as if twitching in the darkness, as he comes.

One time, the woman is on the blackening form coming. It is night.

Coagulating green air with the helicopters thrashing in it shining their beams on the figures tunnels of light appear on the froth.

It's like the tea ceremony. The figures thrash also flapping.

She's lying curled folded and puts his member in her.

Wrapped in the robes which are around them. His member is in between still, and comes with him moving.

Lying on her flat, comes turning. He's flat and invisible. It's night.

The ill man seized in the crowd uncurls.

A tour bus arriving in the afternoon, the crowd emerges from it. Dead Souls is so open she's blurred.

The sumo staggers, the heavy stocks pushing against each other.

From the audience, the stitched faceless leaps and with a switch blade strokes the one sumo releasing his entrails.

The insides pour from him, so that the outer frame is left. Dead Souls's already come to the ring, entering it without thought.

The worm flying to him holds him. The chest gel with the flying worm sucking, the air's rose. She's in the bow clinging to the worm which is quiet flapping.

Being only conscious isn't dreaming clinging to the flapping quiet worm. It's indigo night on the rose air.

She holds the sumo as the worm is eating him there.

If you leave out nature, you can see him dying.

One's on the summer wind holding to the fins of the car. Exhaust surrounds the traffic in a halo. One is kept out of it. The peaceful summer wind moistens her forehead, matting her hair.

The man's opened mouth lying, then curled.

You can see how this is.

The worm flapping is eating the sumo cut rim on the thin wave.

Sumo eaten by the unfolding flying skewered ruffle of indigo air then.

In the white thick air of the heat the child with points for eyes doesn't see in the stream of traffic.

The car goes on leaving her after a while who was just touching the eyeless beating child.

Biting her lip almost up against the glass, the blood comes into the spittle that's flecked her.

next chapter

Holding on to the fender, cars scraped from it, she's in the cornea, the walls, of the beating child who's facing back eyeless, so in a center that is not visible.

In that blank, riding not having motion or sound by being in the dead cornea, she's still separate from others; yet only happens in the cornea not seen.

The sagging husk of the sumo whose entrails have been spilled is in that. That's events themselves.

Events are seen where they're not visible there. To see them only where they're eliminated.

I can make memories occur in this indefinitely.

I don't actually remember her, as that, the face turned over tear-stained, in my own memory. So this is an experiment.

It's coming up solely now. With no memory. City seen from the radio tower that has arcades in it and a wax museum is one. (I went there, so that doesn't count.)

The latter, slumped forward on her desk, dreams of an infant being carried in the mouth of a hyena as it swims.

The waters rippling before it, that could be for something to drink, an ad. That's in her.

See, it's totally controlled. That doesn't matter therefore. I'm not really urgent at all.

Memories are controlled from the outside, but what is solely now isn't.

Centered is the sewer class only.

I want to rid it of that by having it just at that point.

Plots are not in relation to existence. The night isn't. They're crying before they're born. The crowd appears to be on the dusk stream. There's a wavering ball burning in it.

Going to the river to have their bodies or ashes thrown in it to be liberated, they stay in the hospice only if they are about to die, within two weeks.

They have to leave if they don't die then.

In L.A. with the burning ghats around, one just believing and it being rid.

There's no belief system, so that's it.

I'm not at that point. They've seen realistically and it isn't that.

Who's walking through the people shooting up only exists once. If it occurs it's only visible.

A man shooting up in the green air with the helicopter coagulating in it.

Long slow slur of the coagulation of helicopter in it going through amidst the block, there are sleeping forms that don't move in the street.

This is so simple I can't remember it. Saying inside is different from seeing. I've become addicted to writing. I simply can't stop, since for me, it's present-time and the addiction itself is sense of life.

Because the events are not actual and occur. It's the condition of almost not occurring.

I don't know anything. The refrigerator has broken. I guess I'll have to move out.

Just take people off of disability who can't care for themselves, or reduce it, and see what happens.

The folded legs, then like a pear, tremble one time.

The sumo in the ring wiping his hands of the ceremonial salt and swaying heavily to the side, a hippo I met on the path in the rushes with the dawn sky over us eyes cast down, who swerves thunderous into the rushes, the man is similarly early at dawn.

His intestine the jewel sack released, the woman Dead Souls is already without thought entering the ring to him. Akira entered, also at dawn, when this is seen as the mind.

Action isn't the mind yet when brought to its occurrence it is.

Akira is stabbed by the faceless or knitted face at dawn in the rushes, when seen as the mind. Entering the ring Akira with the knifing figure plastered on him is a lung cavity in

next chapter 33

whose cells or cylinders is the blade. Yet at dawn he's carried in the street.

Action isn't the same as one, so it's dawn. Flesh recedes not born, there, but it's only in the other's seeing it. So him blue curled in the dark air is without mind.

The image is subjecting everything to occurrence. This only exists here overtly, clumsily. To subject in love with his flesh to occurrence *per se*.

The hippo met on the path darting aside eyes turned to the side huge on the dawn can't get into being born the bull-rushes are born at a time there. Subject to the dawn.

She withdraws on the long member standing up in her. Then puts it in. She comes.

Turning, sitting up on him.

Surrounded by the people shooting up, he's lying with the eyes gazing downward. She peels back the thin covering to look at him, and the blood has soaked the gauze on his chest which is moving slightly.

Seated coiled sleeping in the plates of armor sockets of quills on the shoulders, no movement on the lidless eyes and yet responds then to the intercepting soldiers. They're attacking for the food and he who's hungry himself sleeping his eyes floating.

Coiled emerges in the plates of armor of quills on the shoulders, his sleeping eyes float.

THE LATTER

I'm Deerslayer.

The handsome head of sumo answers the phone, and since Dead Souls isn't there, Defoe tells him she's going to the

Getty Museum to meet the partner and needs money then to leave. To tell the latter that.

She hangs up, surrounded by the thin film green air. Emerging from the phone booth onto the sidewalk of the street, she goes through a few people shooting up.

The neon signs looming, there's a pool or corridor of quiet underneath, the surveillance helicopter hanging and moving above.

One is just in that circle of beam, so to become very still loosens it.

Not visible in the blank beam of it as hardly moving.

So there's only this. It moves on chasing, with the beam.

What hardly moves in the beam is blank. Anything seen is blank, to be not visible.

So this isn't excitement, excitement itself is stigmatized.

It's a cauterized hole, in which is the small embedded sufficiently shrunken that the rose-jewel intestine is lying on the surface in it, a gel within the rotten frame.

The gel appears to be a deep rose gem in the corpse.

Defoe gazes down at the slender man who's sleeping.

It's burning in the corpse, or rather is a lake.

The man's chest had had the knife plunged in. He's sleeping softly, the sweet breath outside his lips. The latter had extracted the knife instantly fiercely withdrawing it. With the wrestling ring and crowd folding upon him, there's no dream even.

His face isn't moist in fever but almost tender sleeping.

Awake, that's the memory of him sitting at the latter's kitchen table sipping tea and as he's laughing shelling sunflower seeds. He eats the seeds.

He's lying on a cot and in the dim light of dawn Defoe's watching his chest breathe slightly. Our connection to events is existence only.

Leans over him as onto the still lake in which is the jewel.

Chick-the-stick, the greyhound, running to and fro in front of the black waves can't be seen receding except when coming to them and dipping. As if kneeling to the waves coming in, the doe is on the tray briefly.

No days are sustained in the light elation. No worrying comes up in it.

It's not even for itself; itself isn't sustained either.

When it had still been black, the latter's sitting in her kitchen at the table as the police search the place, head protruding from one room and in the hall. She smiles at him graciously, and opens her home to them, the doe-like greyhound rising softly fed from her hand.

Officer says that Akira who's in the LAPD is corrupt and is into drugs.

Bending with the tall frame that's a bow rippling, the officer almost kneels in the ring by the sliced shimmering sumo. One's neither in the bow of one or in the ring. The latter's weeping, the dog touching her.

He's walking on that black air with the long body just gently rippling and the head so high that it's invisible in the air, with the greyhound emerging and reemerging running toward him in it.

Greyhound can't be seen in the darkness and then reemerges its legs folded up on it floating.

Doe-like it moves by his side. His hand goes down his long graceful frame to its head.

Infants being born is unnecessary. Or not being born.

He says he'll accompany her to the races, the silken black hand with very long slender fingers opening the car door. Nervously, she smiles, the doe skittish flicking at her side.

They're pins on the track, with the air up blowing. The latter sits in the bleachers nervously smiling beside the long slender form. That's clouds blasted silently. The greyhounds are almost invisible with no legs in the air.

'Extreme' conflict that was in adolescence unfolding is one serene legless emerging.

Vaulted with no dome sky are pins under it.

Out of that thin air a bimbo woman who is blond set on the rosy limbs and stocks planted in sneakers passes selling hot dogs. The sandy lashes that are a kind of halo under a mass of blond ringlets on a moist parted rose mouth open. Someone's eyes on those which are under the sandy lashes, see her.

They're pins on eyes on those below the sandy lashes which hold open.

Sumo floating on the light surf sags yet it's at night with the round moon up.

So it's very simple to see it separate from the thin day.

The night is in the day. There's no effort to walk and be in the day. They meet. Or not.

While Bechtel's reconstructing the oil fields there's no effort.

It isn't time. Nor am I doing this.

The self is too stable. Compare it. The crowd in the dusk crying has only empty retinas.

In the blazing blue they cry for infants.

Fictionalizing compares to existence openly. The empty retinas of the crowd in the dusk are on burning lily fields.

They reflect the fields. The retinas are burning themselves as are the lily fields which reflect the crowd standing.

They're trafficking in a stream. Their backs are to one another.

Manipulated is solely public itself. I can't find it.

for Jerry Estrin:

Man who's young so it seems the rest of us don't die now oddly. There's no effect to being alive. Why create needless pain by living. At all. Or by dying, for that matter. I mean why is there creating pain by living in the first place or by dying, at all? We have to.

So not living in the first place, yet we live here.

We don't have this pain not living in the first place. Yet here. I see that. I'm going to have to do that.

Why does anything dream in that case? If we're not living in the first place? That was first.

So there's some activity but that isn't living. That's what it is. Some activity before occurs. That's what that is.

In the blue boil the officer furious is a gazelle.

He flies, the slender arms out. He's paying attention to the dark air.

Floating is the worm as such. The night produces it. That is there.

No ordinary life is enough for what we're having.

I want more but it's there.

I love life so much I want only to live. That's wrong as a goal. I don't know why.

The oval opens the black teeth between the lips. A fire storm in the city took her family with hundreds of thousands of others during the war.

Riding in the car, someone else driving, the small yellow cord in one afire floats while it's night.

The yellow cord in one doesn't produce anything. The nerve is on the night, while there, so they're stilled, even. I can see the corpse.

The physical state is endless, as grasped in the light lucidity that was after the operation. That nerve is released from being afire floating in the neck.

The light coming up over the city, riding the bicycle in elation drawing the corpse behind jewel who isn't dead. On the edge of the day one realizes the eyes don't ever see.

One is sitting in a restaurant and oiling down a vodka with relief seeing the worm in the man. It is fantastic inherently and doesn't exist there or on the retina. Or inner. There is no such.

Coming in the night with the legs folded on the body flitting to him in the dark, the officer, dipping the slender hand down to it, balances on his long figure while walking.

It's a warm night and he moves softly in a wave, so that the folded legs up on the body flying to him didn't see him but went out to him where there's nothing from the wrestling ring. It's slung on the warm night.

The long legs unfold from the car and are met by a flying doe with his hand on it running ahead from him.

He says in a low soft voice Souls. She turns in her office smoking at the figure (smoking at it looking but not seeing) of Minnie Mouse on the box. She's calm crossing her legs at the ends of which are small high-heels.

His eyes rest calmly on her and hardly moving with the dog tapping behind him he gazes at a yellow Mercury as he bends going to her blinds.

She nods not even looking at it, the men in the car lounging in the dark.

Her in the blue bow pulling on the gun not even producing his light gazelle's flight to the partner being stabbed, by the flying worm coming to him.

As dying's not produced by someone, that would be just at separation.

Defoe going back and getting the wounded chest and drawing it struggling covered on a litter of bamboo that merely resembles the other street people out carrying all their possessions in shopping carts. That's just what others see.

This is to be the same.

The corpse resembles her but isn't and being drawn by the bicycle lying floats.

The gel's still and illumined isn't seen. That's our culture.

Night in the pea green air.

She leaves the wounded man whose chest is wrapped with bloodsoaked gauze covered in amongst mounds of sleepers on the sidewalk.

They're not moving in the dusk green air.

Corpse follows her walking to the wrestling ring.

A man asks her for money, who's in a silk suit.

They seem like dogs picking.

Yet the corpse is hidden in the crowd which will only move at dawn.

Her companion is even with her. This is entirely ordinary observation.

The thin day with the greyhound coagulating in it barely exists. Dead Souls on her way to the race track the officer on the long slender limbs floats by the coagulating dog. His slender black hand drifts in the air to open the car door for her.

He had been in the previous day with the fleck emerging to him when the limousines wallowing in the air with the sumos emerging coming in for the funeral grieving were rubbed by the crowd.

Dead Souls in the little high-heels comes to the car when there's only thin air with the greyhound floating in it.

To the crowd before dawn, this is like what I dream but it isn't the same thing. Floating, lying, why not? It's only approaching that (what's not dreamed). At dawn the crowd will rise. This has to be of conscious matter. He'll be left there.

In the black the owls swoosh sailing where they eat the frogs. A sweep of them on the 'field' is barely seen as it's night.

To look at one's own death with utter attention at the time of it would be an onus at that moment. Maybe one could just die, more easily. The concentration on one's own death at that moment seems impossible as attentive to the hole neither of which can be sustained.

The foreign workers in Kuwait after fake trials are executed. That's a new poem.

The highest function of the mind is not to have pictures?

The action's so bright that it's infantile.

Sumo emerges in the dusk air.

Sumo carries the man. Greyhound flits in the air by him.

This isn't dreamed. Corpse who's not dead yet is even with the night floating carried by sumo.

He's even with the blue night
being carried and changes.

To be not that
moldering is produced in the blue night then

He is being carried in the blue night by the sumo and a worm in a silk suit flies toward him. Lying in it withdrawing the blade from it. The man in silk suit is sliced in half.

The sumo carrying the coil lying in gel hardly moves walking in blue.

The velvet gelatin stocks with a blue sash in between walk at night, where the man is slung in the sumo's arms. Then floats out, still mounted in the arms, slashing the man in a silk suit who's a worm flying to them.

Before this, sumo at night raises the man up to the dark in the lying bright crowd.

Walking, there's no dark while that's going on. The bright crowd's in dark. Neither exists while one's sleeping.

Between them this man's carried sleeping and uncoils in it to slash the other man in a silk suit who flies up to them.

No rain is falling as it flies here.

Pouring so they're in falling rain when it comes up flayed. That is at the same time.

The flayed man in silk suit is in waves that pour on them, the heavy clothes sagging then.

The blood-red roses thick-petaled rose up fed on the rain. Thick stems on poppies with their black seeds waved on it, since the globe is round.

Yet the thick petals wave off the waving black air. Huge blossoms unfold.

Nothing occurs when one sleeps so one is curious.

The work place is solely work, action is its core supposedly. Action is seen as the secretary thinking she is to serve the employer, that is her job *per se*. They may be debased. That isn't thought.

Looking at the hump ejaculating the black cloud, one is in the night, held.

Sees her on the street, walk as being which is in the corporate world where there isn't any, *per se*. The secretary debases them as the nature of the work place. One has leapt out of one's mind.

The man carried a hump by the sumo ejaculates a black ink in the night. He's a hump as if squid curled in the arms, is just where it's solely alone.

Being public isn't action.

So I'm in it. I would be in sleep also, but not see it. There's no existence of this other than in conscious observation.

The sumo wades in water up to his waist and then up to his arms carrying stick of samurai whom he raises above him in blue night. A hyena begins swimming. Another hyena is swimming in the middle of the water lying on it with a wake of water in a V stemming from it. Chest gel does not unfold as the hyenas swim to him and the sumo. There's no translating this into sleep.

Beaten by a man in a silk suit who was begging, she is lying out.

The indigo night is out and she doesn't occur on it. I write under a pen name.

We're taken into the peaceful rim of nature from what?

The bubble of blue resting, she enters a fury which is only in herself.

They're swimming in rain that's the water, and there's no rain with the worm flying to them who's flayed there. Other events are united to them. Neither can be sustained.

Vertical space swims on deep red. The smear of sun swims. There's no event which isn't seen, so they unite.

Dragging him the limbs float out.

Akira being carried in the rain
where there's no rain
curled in the blue

The burning fields billowing in another waft, open. Akira
is H.D.'s thousand-petalled lily.
figures swim in the black ignited
a hyena swims to them
the light elation is history

The thousand-petalled lily on that aquamarine, a hawk
is flapping not sustained, and drops. Then is flapping not sustained.

These men at a party were backbiting viciously.
They work themselves into a lather of hatred. Ads are the
form of modern spatial sense.
They're to induce seeing nonrealistically what is actually
there: to produce our manipulated perception as the condition
and ground for it.
Cord dragged behind out from woman wandering on the
street in garbage is a rose.

All actions occur there.
Agonizing objectively is stilled
moldering is produced in the blue night
Put people in charge of forests and streams who will
benefit from robbery and pollution.
And a thigh moves from one.

A huge dog hunting me to destroy me turned into myself
in a dream when I was fourteen. That was the first period of
going after myself. I saw my isolated mind at peace outside for
the first time.
Yet the ratlike faceless figures pursuing have no relation
to me or one.

A faceless ratlike figure randomly follows passersby on the street, who're pumped full of bullets.

To base reality of this on it having to be printed in the newspaper, yet this isn't accepted to be printed, the former president is a hyena trotting swiveling with an infant in his mouth then.

He says family values are what is occurring. A businessman beat a woman in robes.

Looking in the indigo night see a worm rising off a man. The man runs in a crowd. Then.

It has no other appearance except in that public form. Yet isn't seen there. Having to be public is the point of madness of what is entirely calm inside.

It isn't itself thus.

Hyenas trotting on the blackened ground in oil drag a woman crumpled in black robes. Another entirely covered with no eyeholes runs with the bristled hyena swiveling lunging with thrust muzzle that tears her robe. The president's wife trotting up disembowels her and runs with the intestine. The others flail at it, then twisting on each other are writhing. Black cakes on them, they're illumined running in the fires.

Like looking at the thin shred of half moon in the blue sky, men in silk suits tear at other slumped figures there.

Soldiers drag a burning person. If this doesn't imitate it, other occurs.

Then a woman down thrashing gives birth.

DEAD SOULS

(I sent an early version of this to six or so newspapers, though it wasn't published, during the election campaign.)

Lyrical horror is our "participation in democracy" at the level of violence of compulsory voting in El Salvador. Taken as an assertion, then, such lyricism no longer works even as a form of bondage between writers.—Barrett Watten

Invisible, not that they're not real, actions occur so that one's seeing has to change to be realistic.

These actions are constantly denied by those in them, though sometimes they are not denied and are corroborated exactly.

So that seeing on the rim one could be free one feels but must see actions on the rim with or as where we live. One links them diverging because that is how to see it.

Unable to walk, there's no way for them to get to work.

Infants don't need to be born.

The eye in the sky floats, liquid, blue.

Silent reading is inner so that it is centralized appearing.

A child is born for delight as its nature. Take fragments of the present. They are not shreds as newspaper text already but modulations of fragments in one.

Extreme is subjective and so not visible in them.

In adolescence in 'extreme' conflict, not a child, one was simply out there. Not needing rebellion even, government not even existing, one was in immunity where the 'extreme' conflict later unfolds and is seen serene outside. Later, as adult one's physical state is endless.

Even greed in the bureaucracy has sunk retentive not appearing to be a motive.

The deaths of infants of a hundred and seventy thousand

maybe in the aftermath of the war are not shown while they force children to be born.

On the edge of the flat, the figure fills the bright blue air. One doesn't have to figure out writing.

The hyenas swarming for scraps are seen on the news, they're the anchormen.

The images do not reflect back. They are only themselves, which is not in relation to existence.

Yet that is existence everywhere. This is to isolate the shape or empty interior of some events real in time so their 'arbitrary' location to each other emerges to, whatever they are.

This is a serial written to be chapters printed in installments in the newspaper, like Dickens' novels. The reader of the newspaper sees in current time. An arbitrary present time image exists in time here. Mimicking here in writing isn't representation.

The leering of the president's mouth on a bulging torso is twisted on pinched haunches as he runs away.

He's going to shoot at them again just to renew his popularity for his reelection campaign.

Thinking is having our original inferior nature. Only sentimentality is communing here. One can't know anyone that way so it isn't communing either. We sentimentalize our killing by wearing yellow ribbons. Not conforming here is the worst mark, being worthy of violence, ridicule for not being valued.

When someone's going to die, so it's repressed in one so as to be sentimental there, that's its occurrence

the one who's not going to die fights hyenas. Scrutinizing is bathos.

So one just imagines that and it's one's life,
the 'groundless' scrutiny.

The boy at sixteen in the Kaiten, a flimsy craft under the sea which could not be steered or retrieved, so that he died by going off into the sea suffocating inside not exploding into a submarine, was not reincarnated as her from his government and people sacrificing millions carelessly, but as utterly free.

Writing is only to be public.

Having deities at all mirrors their government.

The ghouls standing in a crowd crying for infants to be born, their infants are free whether they're born or don't emerge there.

Dead Souls having been impregnated by the president is lying incubating on the lily pond when his motorcade goes by again.

Women who work as a subject is seeing them as subjects.

We can't keep up with being resembled.

Flies fly near her who's floating and carp rise gently from the water catching them.

The president's down on his knees in a car with the head of Exxon.

The war was for Bechtel, the company.

Why do they try to proscribe people's love?

The motorcade is a long line of wallowing limousines in which are the real heads of state, who're from Exxon, Bechtel, and other industries. Some at the same time own the branches of the news media.

Each of these is a chapter. Lying in the gel as if looking down into a rose lake, Akira where the figures are taking crack had said to call his partner at the LAPD to ask for help. Tell no one else he says. The moon comes onto the rose lake.

Akira is not there then, when the moon floats onto the gel.

She goes to a phone booth in the pea stream. The partner had died with the moon floating so without mind.

Faceless ratlike figure holds the partner up in front of her, sticks the blade in between the plates on the older man, for him.

The moon floats on them though it's day when he dies. In the wind coming from the motorcade, some black robes are blowing. The wind is after the motorcade has gone by. The black robes fill flapping like sails. Some of our women, prodded into cattle chutes and harnessed with black robes so that they are veiled with no eyeholes, walk behind the motorcade.

There's consistency in imagery anywhere in it though there appears to be in 'reality.' That's one or us.

A patrician (in) seeing himself as such hangs onto a sense of self (any sense of self is falsity *per se*). At the point at which one's logic is acceptable it disappears, unknown (it is then that place). So there are two unknowns in comparison. There isn't an interior experience as a comparison to the starving people in real time.

There's no rim or bulb of sun on it. Events themselves destabilize in existence, and/or perception of them. Events are translated back into one's syntax as convention itself to be seen there only. Here, we're to 'understand' as sentiment, as if we were the recipients naively. Sentiment in one occurs after an event here. We think we can extinguish images. The hyena floating to one with the infant in its mouth is within their convention, is in itself from existence which isn't produced. Crowds holding their mouths open, it rains. The Sudanese fundamentalist government whom 'we're' supporting is 'allowing' hundreds of thousands of its people to starve in drought by not allowing relief planes for the famine to get through, in order to win the war disputing their group's religious law.

If there were rain actually, there would be no orb on it either. Then the rim itself's eliminated.

A fire that businessmen have started by dropping bombs begins to burn the oil on the surface of the lily pond.

The two lines of comparison aren't separated at all to see what they are.

Our vice president, who links the acceptance of a single mother by the viewers of a T.V. series, which as such is undermining family values to the riots, thinks firing of cities arises from being born.

He should be dumb as cattle.

The image of something real is contemplated as seeing which doesn't exist there. Subject it to seeing which may not ever be its occurrence. Then the image that's real exists solely.

An event is subject to seeing not to its occurrence there. One's seeing it is its sole occurrence.

Where the night and day, which is the dark rim on the ground and blue in the sky, isn't ocular memory. That light sky is subject to dawn, but with no rim.

The handmaiden herself is a tiger who when thrown scraps by the conservative males is enraged in pain.

They run to them in the little steps, so no one touches existence. They can't be living. When they are. Yelling in the crowd.

For a third, two-thirds, of Thailand, babies, men, and women will die of AIDS. Same in Zaire. India of maybe 800 million living will be the main dying grounds, with no medication. Send me there and seeing any standing still living, not dreaming I will bite them.

They touch me in the bow of dusk.

Torn by jealousy I'll bite infecting them if they're still living.

If any are born ever I'm jealous wanting to live and be there with them.

Bombs drop on lily fields, figures float on them. Fictionalizing is separated so that nothing is omitted.

Nothing drops out from fictionalizing, so it examines itself by including.

Nothing occurring scrutinizes itself. We think that.

Fictionalizing is thinking, conceptualizing is our function. The hole of emerging at birth, in the sky of text, isn't sustained here.

Pretence is just that fictionalizing too. It doesn't even waver.

This is in comparisons that are dissimilar so as to have them be peaceful when paired.

Where there's no concurrences, the pair's to be peaceful. (Without psyche fragile or separating in rage—which it does sometimes—as the basis.)

Surprisingly to myself, the writing won't do that. When there's the form of disturbance the occurrence isn't sustained. They're together.

One is in a helpless relation to the rim of nature, which is peaceful.

Newspaper writing has a subject.

It straddles its subject always. It writes on it, in space, it's been eliminated.

A conservative male, who has to have money, has the concept that a subject isn't accurate.

If he's avant garde it's still a subject.

The hyena trotting on the shore slashing at the people as they wade out from the oil on fire comes from (our) fictionalizing. It doesn't have to do with conception. They wade up and are being slashed.

Nature is being socially created yet see it only. It is public solely.

One can drop the pair, but that's where we live. What's that?

Raining, the people standing in it still living, one comes up to them biting to infect them also. Jealous, running at them, who're in the dusk rim being bitten crouch.

My tears are then on a face of a hyena submerged in the air when I'm running.

It's on the red ball a retina.

It makes no difference how one responds as long as there is that. The response, there, has to be increased continually, like some still drug. H.D.'s thousand-petalled lily.

Two days after the operation, waking, itself, isn't sustained in a light elation.

One leans over looking into the pool of chest gel the man swimming in it who's serene and gentle. His eyes floating hanging are closed. One needs him for seeing reality. He's hanging in peace but with one not there.

The man puts his long member in one, bending so he's sitting up on her where the sky's vast and red.

He comes with her in the blue dusk rim which is hanging under the sky.

There's a vast breath on the sky like a blister.

Yet wounded the soft breath comes from him. The response is first. The sky's hot, a blue bowl.

This occurrence in it is seeing, which is the only occurrence sustained. One is to be isolated on the blue dusk rim clear.

It's making a picture of something in order to see it, which is different from simply making a picture: it is between being and becoming so that it is already there. That's objects as history.

Coming out of a bush throwing rocks at the businessmen who're beating and kicking a woman in black robes Defoe is fragile as the black robes has stumbled while running and fallen down still holds her infant.

This is part of their reelection campaign maybe.

It's impossible to have one in an occurrence as being entirely separate from articulation is the condition. That's the moon.

I just realized this writing is passive-aggressive, as a form. If it's on ('seeing') something that's real. It keeps disappearing as the occurrence, as the occurrence does.

This is seeing the shape of events of history subject to that arbitrarily seen.

Analyzing the occurrence that can't be seen it splinters in experience infinitely. It recedes continually, causing infinite pain. *It* isn't even there. People are responsible for the invisible occurrences. That's exciting.

I feel elation at evening, not from it, yet look forward to evening by itself. Not producing in one's life.

On it, after the president's son and myriads of others siphoned money from the public, they wanted it to be placid. That's the media. They're toadying jackals. We don't have words.

I keep trying to make these pairs of dissimilarity hold to be peaceful, as a form. To have occurrence as them at the same time.

Government prods the people into cattle chutes where they are robbed by bankers and businessmen. It's easiest to rob the public by working right at the bank.

Where there are only actions they neither concur nor float.

Actions make the blue dusk rim.

Kuwaiti royalty, hundreds of whose guest workers as itinerant labor suffered from their imperial yoke and in the aftermath of the war were executed with no trials or fake ones, has to pay to go to bed with Bechtel.

That's why the war took place. Bechtel beds Kuwaiti royalty.

As their blue sky is fouled by oil, the pinched haunches of our president beds Dead Souls.

Some of our government officials are drawn from the ranks of Bechtel in fact.

Neither can read. They're made to concur. So the form of the serial novel is that.

The writing is to be as close as possible to nature itself not actually occurring.

Writing is just mechanical: the condition is clear, as one *is* in sleep when not dreaming.

The sumo low scuttles forward on huge crouching legs and pats the other one. There's no content. The open palms slap and slap from the crouching scuttle on the other sumo's chest. One rushes forward with the weight mounted down on the almost kneeling huge legs so that only the palms move in the blows. His haunches scuttle gently.

This is pushed to where being is narrative solely, contentless.

There is *no* angel running toward one which is the same as resting (not) coming to one in the blazing blue.

They're set in the base of their bodies. Crouched in the setting of this powerful lower setting as base, they come out fighting from it, not where *they* are.

Which could run very fast, from it being weight. The black butterfly in the blue has no weight, and the blue doesn't.

A government can't simply be a business for profit. Then it drops out the people lying on the street who are the inner self.

Schools are not simply businesses but are to cultivate the inner self.

We don't have words at all.

As if sealed in the rose dawn, the first lady runs with the wieners. Her hind legs shaking, she's pulling them out of a woman. That women are to be in the home humbling themselves, who really have to have jobs out of necessity, is uttered by the (former) first lady as her hind parts are shaking when she pulls.

Our (former) vice president tries to turn us against the "cultural elite." Here, the cultural elite are simply people who can read at all.

That's a new poem, as seeing being taken to its first surface.

NOW

Walking on the sailing quiet pillars with the red ball in the stream, I went on the floating deserted road toward the dissolving frames around me everywhere crumbling afire in the black air.

I'm a scout on the quiet road into it.

That's hanging on the world driving on the cliff in evening, so the entire ocean is in it, the outside eye that looks at it from elsewhere, not from oneself, isn't connected to it.

And it is not mine. The deserted road on the rose rim can be brought to separate.

Street people still begging as the rose rim separates are on the street.

This gets to where the eye isn't mine. While seeing, it's elsewhere gazing quietly.

The guest workers executed for sympathizing with the foreign invaders occurs now under the jurisdiction of Bechtel. It quells them to have order.

There isn't existence except ahead of them. Bechtel now works them where there can be no unions.

In the comparison itself is a range. Real time and fiction actually conflate on the rose rim.

They are the same.

To bring writing to a point where vision occurs, to actually see there physically, it is not from one.

For example, a man seeing isn't the blue eye floating in existence.

This is to where seeing comes from or in the events produced. The outside eye floating on its own sees the man gently put his stem in her.

One is a blindspot which begins at the mouth. As in Lori Lubeski's corpses aroused, intrepid, moving alone, *no* world is from her strong boyhood dream.

Lubeski's "The bloodhound eyes / inset a criminal mind forever the capillary": dream causes space for the mind criminal to be amused. It is the Persian Gulf, our country.

It gets to where nature is being seen as originless. It is by itself. Aaron Shurin's "Human Immune" hallucinates nature. As if it were blind.

Our being opposed to analysis is the means of seeing from in the dim blue boil.

One isn't being it when the fin amidst the people.

So the image is in nature, and we're not, we're a habit. The image is its own outer realm.

Others are the image 'only,' as if it were just being induced.

Shurin induces it. It's a double erasure.

If he induces nature or the image, where they're not separated, there's the man amidst the people being a fin—'in order' is seeing it as originless.

That erasure 'culturally,' which is everyone's, and as literally death of 'others' from AIDS is the act of realistic hallucination in his "Human Immune." Being in that space of 'everyone's' is akin to enmeshing of Robert Grenier's 'poem' which he drew in handwriting "I am a beast / my heart is beating," the two lines inextricably superimposed on each other visually. It can be only what we see, not translated as type (of printed letters). Nature is writing as drawing (or can be type).

Whereas in some of my writing I would take a series in time of real events as 'their' 'ostensibly' constellated interiorily, and at the same time as it being that see the events being constructed by the social order (which is then seen and changed interiorily, in the writing); in this, the narrative is only.

The narrative is frontal, solely.

My interiorily is the same as or superimposed in the social construction in it. In the 'narrative' it doesn't exist.

The 'narrative' is divided but isn't within one.

Formerly, one had to be interiorily at odds in *both* of two cultures and so be a child to mirror that.

The 'narrative' is where nature is almost not occurring in people being pressed to, compared to, while being in dusk.

Where the foreign workers are now to work for Bechtel in Kuwait is a poem, which is real time itself. *Per se.*

Real time is produced by events. Only.

If the image is not dreamed but is on the edge of its occurrence *it's* not dilated.

Apprehension is so close it produces and can't see. That's the eye hanging. It's mine.

In a play, the characters will say the passage of themselves through the landscape because the eye is not in them—by nature being hallucinated by one who is watching.

A man seeing Jean Cocteau's *Orphée* saying it frightened me tentatively yet inured says I'd never paid attention to content before. He sees behavior as convention everywhere except the physical wilderness.

Why *isn't* this some humans' seeing?

There are no people: but that condition has to arise here not from people. Only, or has no people.

Robert Grenier's drawn superimpositions of a drawn phrase in one color on another phrase in some other color (so it's only its visual being) are the actual horizon line on the edge/ meaning of the written poetic-line. Which may not 'exist' itself in the writing (line breaks of poems not existing, where there's only the physical line of drawing).
Nature has no line either.

She can't wait while she's bruised. In the bruised Defoe walking on the street expands the blue sky.
Defoe's kneeling on the blue blood sack, which is her own chest as if a bird.

Beaten by the man in the silk suit who was begging, one floats up and is on the crust. By one. A culture can shimmer.
The silk suits are floating up in front as out on the street one slumps bruised blue surrounded by them who're coming up.
Concealing being bruised a sack sees, them, who're not existing there nor does one then. One doesn't move on the street in it.
The tips of the grass are purple waving in a sheet where I looked up and saw the moon hanging in the bright blue.
Further on the sheet the tips of the grass are black. Black waves blew toward me.
A woman with empty retinas comes up with her mouth flecked. One isn't reflected. She's saying one not being like them is ridiculed in this arising from one's self-confidence. One isn't reflected anyway. How does she see them?
So one'd have to have no confidence to see her. One has none.

A cord red crusting it a bulb on the end is an outside's beet. That grew strewn in the outside unattached, a camel's inner cord.

Sealed in the blue bruise grapefruit-of-one's-flesh is a blood sack outside of one's eye.

If they live it they can say it. It's still, not moving in the dim blue of a day, existing there. The silk suits aggressively bawling at the empty retinas are in this narrow blue boil outside where she's bruised in the black night.

The jet of the black ink ejaculated from the floating man curled, he speeds forward with no effort in him through the dim night.

He is without her. As if we're attached like sacks that stop breathing. They don't see one at the moment. She pumps on her back in the night, in order to walk.

That's when what's here no longer reflects. It's neither in the present or memory.

No rebellion affects it. There is no suffering in not being like them but rather in being so. The ridicule forces the crowd into a bright herd. One, who're all, is forced back into quietness. Ridicule can't affect one. It's a quiet bubble of calm in them in which they reflect as rigid and brutal to themselves.

They're wearing yellow ribbons sobbing to themselves still.

The man jets on his own sack on the black ink cloud from it where there's no horizon or night.

Akira who is him clings to the worm in the air. Saying pear-eyed to her he'd been rowing with a friend seeing fins, he says to him they're sharks but the friend comes very close to immense sea lions. They're basking on the water. Turning as one to the boat they fart to the men.

So Akira leaning drinking a whiskey over the walk g-strings going by on the sand in the day, later when he's lying in his own gel says that to her meaning not to go to the Getty.

The fins were incandescently tranquil before from the herd then turning as one to fart suffocating the men.

As Dead Souls is speaking to the men who're there to buy,

inside the office, inside her sockets her steely gaze sees Defoe outside far off on the street.

An osprey flies under the crescent moon flake in the bright blue right now.

Here they float in front diving. Whang one drops on the thin surf rim where the air's dim with blue.

The entire range of events, of others and one, is occurring on conscious apprehension not dreamed. That is their only existence though we're not in them. To be just there in their rim is not being asleep.

The neons and the ads everywhere mechanically make the image, the same as this. The dusk is not subjected to the ads.

One isn't qualified by the dusk or on it.

The dusk is turning a dark blue as one is bruised in it. Whatever the men begging think they're illumined. They can't not. Is that the same as the dusk? It can't not.

As the dusk rises and a deep velvet pool of dark settles, the silk suits are on a boulevard. In that relation is my existence.

Crowds who are lying down on the sidewalk to sleep, don't look at her. The space has no pressure.

That's morning at the dark pool of night, where they're together—they don't have anyone in them. A dog is the rose dawn later. Moving by her.

O Blind World: that's day itself. Brown velvet cattle float quivering to one. Singing had to be invented by humans rather than simply being as it is in birds.

Maybe we began with it.

There we expressed tenderness for the animals.

The fury is only in her. Rose dog that has it in it doesn't produce it. One was gutted inside lying unable to sleep, fury when a man's died, as poured in the dog which doesn't feel that or derived it itself, there.

The latter is sitting in her office smoking bowing waiting on some men. She never takes drugs.

They are brutal buying are in a helpless relation to nature too, which is the dawn or light even. That's not the dawn on dusk pressed independently. We have to perceive that there.

What's the difference? The people on whom she's waiting are minor so she has to oil them, a tyranny of servitude arising from wanting to stay alive.

They're taking cans of peas.

The wrestling ring ahead in the pearl night is produced by it. One's bruises are blue in the night. One doesn't reproduce violence in such an event.

In Charles Bernstein's poem "Circumstraint" a terrain is flattened to be simply reading, as of Dick and Jane in first grade, so that by neutralizing as if numbing that landscape a 'gaze' (rather than a consciousness, which is more—or less?—programmed) is really everywhere in it, not from one's self—the dropping (at the same time) of its own double negative space of "Nowhere seen / Nowhere withheld."

> Dick runs, run, running
> out back clear past (the range.
> A plan for complacent relegation,
> denuded of song or story.—*Only*
> *what unleavens dwells at adjacency,*
> *the blind behind the melt.*

That's not song or story, *it's* a blind eye as real time, by its having no disruption or revelation as modulation of feeling. It's because it's blind in back, but doesn't have song or story as it either. It's the 'neutral' place. The gaze isn't seen anywhere. The text is then as such this/our real time.

The neutral nuance registering a reverberation there (yet dependent in its articulation), they're impermanent.

A moth the dust smudging from the wings yet in a very violent hot blue air.

That he would accept weeping
When one's in the blue blister in the night—sitting—and he comes flapping.

and he's completely unknown to one
base the night (there) on that—and war.

While there is no neutral range (maybe there is?) in reality, this 'neutral place' which is observation of reality is only in the writing. The ranges are without 'our' credibility?
Custom isn't a norm (in nature), objective. It is.

We try to find the swans in the day that has no weight.
That's the day.

Flashbacks so that everywhere people seemed to be seen. They were bleeding through at this time in the street.
Holding to his warm chest flapping in the oily dark, it wasn't touched actually or there.

The space now is such that a horned roiled (figure) has no origin, is entirely the foreground, floating on flesh-hued cloud.
That background is here, the horned roil does not arise from it.
The demon floating has no origin, spatially. Spatially is emotionally here. I want to subject emotion to space; and also to subject observation to it.

Wanting him as real as can be only in this and with no death, Defoe has become Orphée.
Orphée was originally Defoe.

Mist didn't fall on that desert. The figure withering aging could not be.

Yet showers from the plates of cloud fall on the desert. The utter happiness of love for Akira on the illuminated blue field is, yet one has not existed.

A child is sticking its arm down the throat of a calf, several calves lined in the street. The child sticking an arm down its throat, feeding the calves, there is no middle ground here. They're silhouetted.

The calves don't utter. There's no silence in that. They don't, in it.

There's no sky. The faceless worm is the same as the child and calf attached at the child's arm. Feeding the calves is in this.

The approach to find another civilization is not seeking historical knowledge. One has not existed.

Akira being in death is akin to the nerve in one which feeds the flesh telling it to remember to be alive. Otherwise the flesh is in rigor mortis while the person is still living. She experiences this in her own flesh first. The utilitarian world is lost but it is not missed. The nerve is the "Word" in the flesh, as in the captions, lettering as such, coming from angels' mouths, early cartoons.

What is the relation of words in dreams or awake to the nerve in one telling one's flesh to be alive without which it forgets?

This text must be literally the instructions to physically live. What does that mean to what occurs *while* living?

No one sees this. It is Frankenstein in reverse.

What causes the nerve in the neck in one to be alive at all? One would have to cross past the line of the word and flesh, a state of they're not being. Where there is only real death, extinction.

The tree(d) (as of it, not the past) apple-blossoms are the same thing as itself yet not enflamed in it. Spring blossoms loose (as being there in it—at all) not enflaming people.

In a deep sleep, so that waking setting out in the car no orientation being found—in utter extinction (extinguished sockets in bright air—though not breathing in the black thorax then either, breathing in the upper chest as if running and utterly quiet) of no cognition yet seeking to re-form the structure seen before, which wasn't being resumed—the magnolia buds opened in a thin blazing blue.

Aware muffled that one needn't seek the structure yet is doing so, struggling lumbering. One waits to be clear only to find it (there being an opportunity not to be in it), yet there was no pairing in it—none possible in utter heavy disorientation—the magnolia cups 'occur' only in the bright air there.

No elation even is close to it—or at all.

People meeting in an occurrence by acting something else as if pressed to it momentarily, its reality is coming from various people by their not speaking or acting which is that event, but rather, their being as separate as being it. It is occurrence only with people.

But that impermanence does not stop the other from dying. It is therefore as close to that state as can be.

Then too,
others being willing to grant a 'life' as having significance (based on being in a group, or having such-and-such affiliations)
as opposed to being nothing—one, only—as spring, there.

'Pride-riding' of one's black thorax—only—as if isn't a 'life.' (In oneself doing it.) Aware of her, someone else, resting on authority (of a relative or group), 'there isn't even the blue in which one is' in physical fact. One has to 'allow' in one's conception (as being one's impermanence) him to be impermanent utterly.

The branch of apple-blossoms as tree(d) only in air—and people meeting as motions that are not the same as the event occurring which are being their meeting—not enflaming and in it—(and not enflaming:) as one being 'oneself' there—one not having to resume anything

At his brother's funeral, taking his turn speaking in memory—saying again the old family notion (in him reincarnated from his father, him reincarnated in me), of his own being inferior as introverted which by that in him is sensitive comprehending, wholly free in protecting others as sublimated—which he compares as inferior to the brother being daring as 'gregarious'—when is oneself?

(So that—later defending him my saying "we" don't have to be that, 'gregarious'—"we'll" be doing something else—him almost stopping me for defending yet hearing the word "we," as only there deliberately, him comprehending as on one's own ground, is one then being free to be there—)

The apple-blossoms as tree(d) yet (as:) in air—(as if their jetting)—(yet as not from existence)—and their being there, as the only opportunity (of one—ever)—and in being oneself not from cognition

The number of beings where those motions in conflict were being made, yet that not being one, is the same as stars seen during the day

(for example: the number of beings in the one place—of living or of one's birth, then, seeing mimicry of war, as if blossoms-tree(d), which is elsewhere yet is as motions there where one is, as if it were one—after the schism in one as extreme conflict which is later serene in that one yet there—is the opportunity of being there as being from no cognition)

(as in that 'conflict'—not one—of apple-blossoms: tree(d)—(as) which is—being—yet only in spring)

A man sitting exhausted on the sidewalk in the crowd has

running bloody sores on his bared legs, holds a cup. A sign beside him says he has AIDS. They're in the warm sunlight.

It's the same as their impermanence. He speaks in a humble way. Their living can't occur being articulated in any tradition. There can't be 'tradition of one's faculties' even.

That action is all that's happening. Tapping, the greyhound was by him in the blue air. Dead Souls who goes off up on the stadium to the blasted sky the clouds float over. The officer is paying for the hot dogs holding them, comes into the garden at the Getty. The officer, who is in the air ahead of her, glinted teeth at her. She's firing at the faceless worm a ratlike puckered figure on the dead man. They're out in the blue air only. The same blue air of the stadium. The officer was angry with the woman.

Yet he knows the deaf and blind child in the limousine is hers.

The neutrality as if words are stilled there to be 'their' medium is objective as if in *no* terrain and as if one's opal companion.

Akira sitting out drinking whiskey looks at a black butterfly by him in the blue air. How can he see it?

It's in the air so can't be seen then.

Kneeling deer where they've made hollows there bedded in the field *aren't* beside her. It is a habit.

That's why one doesn't want to die.

It doesn't see oneself. A man, which appears, curled, ejaculates the black inky cloud not to move.

Not to see *as* seeing. That's what it is.

In my writing, this being written now is a modulation visibly moving as if 'behind' 'in' the terrain; and there is no image while it is going on—it could be the earlier eye or not.

The nerve is the word in flesh, forgotten in rigor mortis. One revived fully would go past what we call 'life.'

Breathing on Defoe's blue face, one of them flies to her looking. They're on the night or appear to be. There's no violence reproduced anywhere in life; where structure is simple.

People are sacks of blood beating like bats. They both walk, the silk suit on it a bead bursting to her whether *it's* dawn or black, from what?

One's heart swells, really the chest gel sees the night, or dawn. We don't cause anything. That's exciting.

The blood sack is floating on the night.

The self is too stable. I'll have to not do anything to see dawn.

Dead Souls waiting until the people have left and then putting ice on Defoe lying in the bruises, while Souls, an entrepreneur, draws the curtains first that are like bulbs blasting, opens her blackened teeth in rims as she looks out at night briefly.

She smokes caustically at the night.

The sound of the street being trashed rises.

Souls smokes at the blinds flat on the lights of the city. She flattens distinctions scrutinizing not caring for it, that's not in thinking of anything, without forms. A tree covered by the wilting fur lone in being blighted, sprays not visible to the open eye surrounded on the emerald fat vegetation floating. She laughs bitterly really nothing there it's so known. It's kick-started. It flashes bitterly where she eliminates that burning it. Smokes caustic on it it's so open dilated. She ground on it so that there's nothing floating. On what isn't there not caring. Before she'd seen it as it's on the open eye burned then, not hers.

We feel the need to unite with where one lives but we never are there (the rim on the neck cut sumo floats); it seems that without his gel cavity (the quill soldier's being carried— so this is inducing dying) one would be separate from it for that instant. The only time one sees it.

The image as it is writing is eliminated. To view action from innocence makes their view that content is sentiment. View innocence from action.

Nor is action a view when there is the image. There isn't any view here, even that of not having any. Thought doesn't see innocence or action.

The man running infected biting in the crowd as if a fin floating through it seen on it isn't in thought and isn't in sentiment. Thought has none of the effect of sentiment, yet it isn't in the suppressed physical state.

Which also sees. Groundless scrutiny is our wilderness anyway. If physical seeing isn't it solely, there's no innocence rather than sentiment that is occurrence solely.

They merge as if a fin in the crowd. The man is solely the fin in it.

Deerslayer is a point of view the fin only, and so is extinguished by observation on it. Innocence being occurrence solely can't be a point of view.

Kneeling on the blood sack as if it were a robin's breast can only be seen as an image in one. It's isolated.

A dream in the middle of the day was impinging trying to break through to be my conscious day activity; standing there, I couldn't really remember it, though it was or had been frightening. I'd had no awareness of it or when it first occurred.

I was having a 'psychotic' experience. One is seeing a shred clearly while being in a healthy state, they're in a blue dim floating.

I was in it, as it was in shreds, with it going on at the same time I'm standing being in an ordinary activity.

There's no sense that it arises from suppression of the physical state with cognition not really existing in it.

If cognition is entirely occurring in the state of a sort of suppression which illuminates a real sky horizon

it isn't cognition producing the dream.

The dim blue burning softly occurs again, every day.

That's why it being groundless not being other than its

occurrence can't be seen here other than an image. Action is extinguished. So is outside of real time, is groundless scrutiny.

Is culture itself. So is sentiment an image. We don't 'participate.' It is the only 'joy of life.'

This fiction is to apprehend this real time. And change it merely by that, by *it* being outside.

What is it?

The physician says, in one having decided to have the operation on the nerve, to go ahead simply.

To know what could go wrong is irrelevant.

The blood sacks beating are in comparison to the blue air. I want to pair them which haven't serenity in themselves, and that is what's here. A balance is in one. Not making something serene.

The eye in one isn't turned inward. Insofar as one is the image being observed and is the observer, and so there is no image—here the eye isn't observing itself, and so itself doesn't exist. Yet it is here.

The blood sacks dragging in the blue air, some people don't ever feel balance. People running, if the self is too stable it can't see the real.

The very words used to convey their reality are fixed so that the syntax can only be that same view. To translate another language is to change it to their convention.

Life is their place, as if one can only go back to it from a place that is after where they are.

The image doesn't have a cause or origin that exists. One's not being on nature.

Events are conscious on the blue bead. She is isolated in the blue bruise in the night.

The images are in one that is dead in the sense of not retentive, while one is alive. It's the limitlessness of no memory.

This is reproduced mechanically only because it really exists. When she's lying bruised blue in the blue boil that's all the present.

There aren't memories there.

I've brought this to the point of where it can't produce anything. The connection to where one lives isn't produced and goes on.

An ill man thin breaks running into the crowd yelling at night. The crowd scattering frayed, he appears to chase one and then another running and then crosses his own course aimlessly. In the dense crowd people slowly scatter which doesn't affect the outside of the crowd.

He comes too near the silk suits, one shooting him as he tunnels into the crowd away from the clinging band of ratlike faceless ripples in indigo.

One's limbs go out. Crumpled ripple of the flat man comes to the edge of the crowd as it passes by him.

Flat is riding on the bead. He's looking down into the bursting moving bead.

NEW

Akira's lying on the black air of dawn. Being in the crowd that is curled on the sidewalk is on the rose line of dawn where there's no perception. Ever.

The chest gel is bared as a glowing worm in the crowd set in the man flat whose limbs are stretched, or rather not themselves but hanging out floating from him in the rose air.

He's just there new, in the black air, so that it's sealed on the rose rim, the only place here.

In the burning lotus fields on water the hyena is coming to them. Swimming, the head just submerged into the black rose rim of air. It doesn't swivel but barely moves. The fires around the hyena are ignited but don't give off light, rather the air they're in reflects or creates it.

It's a dense medium. Sunk in this air, they may create it. The heavy pans of the helicopters sinking and rising go by.

The crowd is underneath on a stream. Prostrate floating submerged in the air with the hyena, they have no faculties and that may create it.

The sumo handsome head swaying on the stocks bends. There's a wide bow in the air.

He bends over emerging on the rim.

Lying on the street is at the bottom of dawn, resting there so it's just thinking that.

The rose light so that he's on the rim holding the man, the sumo picks him up in the black air but begins moving bounding like a vast bulb floating on it.

A worm flies to them on the street. The air unfolds in the silk suit softly billowing to them faintly in it. As it meets them, the man held by the sumo swims out slashing it. His projecting from the arms of the sumo, they're buoyed so not from each other.

The green hump lies peacefully no eyes floating on the sky.

Eyes closed floating, gazing downward inside, on the rim of dawn he's slashing swaying out at the worm flying to them then.

To the sumo, as it flies to them, sealed in the air, this appears in the purple as skewered ruffled billows, flattened and dead so as to only be in the widened air.

That's floating in it where the rim is lost too.

I can't find the relation to this.

But one would have to loosen it utterly to pick up on the dusk air that's on dawn.

One's not in that, so can't exert force to find it. Or floating on it is on the occurrence, where there's no forcing going on.

Seeing what we all see is floating on the occurrence.

Where only some diverging from it, emerges on our actual air. Actions only are the occurrence. Any could be not dreamed.

The point of reading is just to read, *per se*, so that real actions are submerged in our air. They're on the blue, bulbous air, inflated.

But I can't myself not dream. When I'm asleep it's a deadened blank sometimes but that's not it. I just have a small life. I want when asleep to be while awake (seeing when sleeping is not to ever sleep) to eliminate this.

That is having the eye floating in the sky. And the hyena comes up to it swimming. It is not on my eye.

The wildly coagulating heavy sides of the helicopter go over again so that those underneath crouch in the pea air where the sumo carrying Akira in it flaps.

A larger range has been opened on a horizontal frame where the sumo flaps in the dense coagulation but so thick they're not moving in the beam which only reflects the pea stream.

The jewel that is this abandoned intellect on it was never abandoned elsewhere. That isn't him.

There's no eye floating. That's in Akira hanging down now, the sockets hanging are carried. His comforting presence is still calming as long as he's living.

No one's a function for being calm yet without him the dissimilarities on the pea stream are held and aren't peaceful (when living). That's interesting. The pea stream narrows a track to 'natural' death, what else is there, while before it is society, yet having any concept is inaccurate where something occurs. On it.

So there's only the occurrence on the stream with him

or being utterly lost, as if there were souls, and one'd known him.

He'd had to be born. Same as the rest of us. That's good.

But now one is a fool isolated, from him, in frozen society which is like a blister here. One looks and there's a blister on one's skin, the head swiveling. People go by. In a restaurant, they stare out.

Nothing happens but that.

The hyena floating to one.

She sits quietly at a cafe looking at the thin air with it in it.

Just seeing them, who is calm when he's still living, is only encouraging.

A freeway overpass chokes the ball in the blue air, swirling as an eye itself when one glances, the changing air.

If it were the hyena it would swim coming up with the fetus between its mouth as it did.

They'd meet.

Not to exist eliminates the blue boil. It's him, not oneself there.

The fat flowers bloom in the dark.

The crowd pulses by her in blackness when she sits at the cafe with the flowers opening around her. She'd seen them in the past, then.

She sees the people in the cafe come up and would be separate from him alive lost.

In their view, one's actions 'are composed,' passively, being a narrative connected that illustrates, rather than being in existence.

He floats in the black on his own ejaculated stream.

seeing one's decomposing sack of flesh playfully

Sitting oiling down a vodka at the cafe, where he had once been seen, in their view the actual world is symbolic and permanent, a higher authority 'giving' meaning to 'scenes' (decomposing having meaning).

That is why, without him, one feels being mocked.

No matter 'how' one sees motions that 'appear' to be connected, the motions will be seen (by them) to reassemble the 'picture,' of 'their' reality (by which the motions are interpreted).

the sack of one's body is its changing composition (decomposition) which is without authority, even decomposition

events are floating in a sole existence, having no other manifestation
from being produced in the series

so one has to be a nomad to
continually engage one's decomposing self
without 'meaning' and so in actual existence

The sumo is sitting with his back to Akira, a lying hump.
The sumo is upright with his legs hanging in front his back a slab gazing at the ocean, on the sand.
The green rim swims with their being before it. The sumo is quiet inside, with Akira rotten oozing chest lying as a hump behind him peacefully.
There's 'groundless scrutiny.' There's no ground.

At the cafe, the green hump floats before her jetting up on hanging on its black cloud.
It is in the blue.
Hump oozing wounded can be seen in it.
The black cloud hanging, a stream behind him in the blue is seen.
A starry sky is faced in which the emerald green hump is swallowed when at night. Another time, people leaving the cafe go out.
Night is this scrutiny not quieted by the burning blue.
The hippo turning away on the dawn path is in mind so being quieted it's seen barely.
The samurai hangs lidless to the dawn.
One's teeth are clenched so it cannot be at dawn. It is sleeping.

As such, jetting at night when he's just coming to it, as if coming and turning away in a tank.
The dawn's just there, and he's just come to it, reaching to it. That seems to be that he's not moving when just at it.
Beggars here so numerous it's like Calcutta.

When I'd actually been on the path the pear-eyed hippo veered off it.

The actual times cannot be there even when he's existing. That is when he's still existing.

Why am I worried? I'm still existing. Being in 'extreme' conflict in adolescence is later serene 'existing.'

I'm still up so close.

I'd walked on the street in Paris at dawn a wide boulevard, but a straight street that crossed the entire city at rush hour, the straightness being itself the track. So it's not the city itself.

That's the only place where one can live.

The soldier standing does not make the hanging eye. It's an outside eye. The mind finds our wilderness. The intellect finds it by the movements occurring before it. Existence is in the movements only. One is in it only consciously.

One time she'd come up.

The sumo floated away the pinned up hair seen, going back to the wrestling ring.

Yet swimming on him, she finds him, the sumo rolling on the wave the back of him quiet. She's in the heavy bed of water the limbs below her flicking slowly over the bottom and is entangled with Akira.

The hump churning in the water, he bursts up, but then is down floating underneath somehow.

Actions are collapsed onto one horizontal frame. That's bathos.

The waves are indistinguishable on his green hump wallowing softly.

One time, he puts the long member into her. Venice Beach washes a long way off.

There's only one rim.

The hump curled over her, but with the member stiff out; he puts the member in her.

The green hump coming, he then sits up on her after. He's looking out in the blue air. She comes flat, in the sand, and he takes the member out of her.

Lying in the gel, she holds him.

On the sand, the red chest gel is seen with her sitting up on him in the blue air.

Maybe uniting with events that are somehow on the stream of the present because one thinks that is living isn't indicated. What if these events never touch the rim that's living?

As if occurrences were that one struggled to be in war and death? This is what *others* think, that one shouldn't unite with it. Maybe the dark opal companion is one's living.

The long stream opens and one's opal companion is lying in it awake so it's necessary to unite there, while he's living.

The *physical* life is non-existent, by occurring from suppression, but is occurring by itself.

'One's' only existence is in conflict *per se*; so that conflict is outside. It's only there moving.

The union is the only 'self' when there's not one. Why is the being of 'one' conflict solely?

The one can't appear, by itself. Yet Akira appears.

Sometimes it appeared by itself. If one is without conflict it isn't the same thing (as one).

If it is not oneself's orb (that which is *only* conflict) one is continually transgressing it in the conflict. This occurred in the past of my youth.

Wanting to cling to Akira in existence is one which is in it again 'by itself.'

Seeing existence *outside* of Akira, so that he floats, is existence itself occurring.

The bodies of the men in the night were backs and buttocks with the heels seen pinned as if they were black butterflies (in it).

Moving, yet almost still flapping, in the black

In the bright blue day, the men were seen with only their

backs hunched gills as if grey their heels pinned as they walk as if there also a black butterfly in the blue.

Because it's blue.—So not dependent on the night, as their existences aren't dependent in it or in day.

They were moving beyond their dying which hasn't occurred yet anyway, by the day having them in its blue.

The black butterflies, which are only night can't be in the blazing blue.

A man vomits the blazing blue when he's black butterfly still flapping in it.

The street is a glazed place.

The yellow cord in one's white lacquer apparently observes

the conflict that one was only 'one,' transgressing that is not that conflict,
one sees that conflict only in its being in the series

that one is or was conflict solely
separatable from existence is only its place

One didn't believe in that place, believe that conflict then or see it but can see looking back in Creeley's series
in *their* being only chronological
in the collection of series

The lacquer white flesh floating immersed on its yellow cord
the cord in one's white lacquer observes?
one is seeing through the slats of the train window the lotus fields bogs with dark pigs in them
The besotted pig on the blue seen floating by the pad, wide emerald pads floated on the field, bog, is real occurrence
and so close to death by being outside

Far away, Akira jetting, is a crescent moon.
form barely effecting it
it's not 'inside' if it's the non-dreamed state
(I'm not interested in death.)

A musculature beating in order to breathe, the beaten burning sack opening and closing, the heavy muscles swaddling the delicate rib cage, closes. One lay submerged within (barely breathing not in the thorax, in the general anesthetic).

because it's the minor still flitting in the basin, one sees the physical body has no end

The purple black musculature is beaten within.

The man comes up with no legs them curled on him in the roiled night.

A figure vomits a black ocean yet standing in the black air.

The heavy rain hitting in waves that waving up from the street, people huddling in doorways having run in troughs and lightning hitting around one when one crossed to them, one breathed the purple clear roiling air.

Akira, carried by the worm silk suit billowing on it, as it had fed on him in the air

had come up floating, had jetting in the night to it

which at night one figure vomits a black soft coagulation in which the man comes up jetting hanging.

Ringlets on the moist brow bent on the hams crouched flying, the golden heavy thighs of the bimbo pumping through the air on a bicycle, a curled figure, is in the basin.

The bimbo shoots into the basin alone in it—the heavy blonde thighs that shoot crouch in the air. The moist panting like bellows steaming crouched on the tires skidded to a blackened stop, as she looks back from on the bicycle.

Dead Souls having been told by handsome head that Defoe will go to the Getty and needs money is the informant to the glittering limos, which wallowing in the night produces the figure emerging from a limo coming to meet the fragile dew-like Defoe in the garden. They're brought into the mother-of-pearl day. Dead Souls who stepping into the ring had held off with her arm the flapping worm, blood drops from her arm—while she thinks

"Transgress by knowing and narrow to the blue night in it."

One's spinal nerve as entering to where it's only centered is a place where the one can exist limpid, elated.

She enters the morning on the boardwalk with the grey-hound chick-the-stick roiling to her passing out of sight.

The bimbo on the bicycle glancing on the skidded blackened skid, steaming turning back sees in the blue.

The flapping in the ruffles of silk suit far away, flaying in the blue night, narrows to it

emerges into the dark blue horizon with one who's seeing as we are not to exist in turmoil

where the live cornea relaxing in it is missing the flaying figure skating to one in the light blue night

the worm figure floats to one in the dark where the vast light blue night is behind it

They're just shooting the supporters of the young president (martyr if he returns), not a political leader, when they come out at night sitting in cafes, openly. The supporters are defenseless.

They will simply kill him if he returns which is groundless—as the butterfly that can't be in the blue air—because the air's blue—which isn't scrutiny.

Another figure vomits a dazzling blue
a floating worm on the hot air
comes up killing figures in cafes at day

The series is secular in a sole existence, its chronology.

There's no consistency in the series so it is only its chronology

Now it is not 'one' as being itself conflict, only (which existed before, and is now unknown).

When one is the middle child, soon the person isn't there.

If actions make the blue dusk rim, one's not dropping the paired rim there. Companions are occurrences and if there were 'souls' he's one's. So it's the green hump on the rim burning in blue.

The hump smeared is the rose line that's the wave of night. It's hardly apparent.

The heat beginning at dawn.

The hump wounded sitting, the slab of back turned from Akira on the sand starts off into the vast crackling ocean. The sumo is held in a wave.

Plowing in the black water there's no indication of the sumo except him seeing with the beads.

The various places of attentiveness here have 'no' counterpart still by not being repressed. They are not repressed anywhere. It's a 'wilderness' (there isn't that).

Though they don't see what other people see they create it. They make that congruence of their imposition, even of not seeing it.

The sumo with the lacquered hair pinned up floats with his quiet back away along the horizon to the ring.

Rung of waves swell where the sumo's going adjacent to the plate; he's away while at the wrestling ring her blackened teeth open with a red rim around the oval. The black painted clouds on the forehead, she's kneeling in the ring. Something's moving on her knees swaddled in the robes.

The quiet back floats to her.

Pursed ruffle on the bright blue, merely the pinched butterfly of the legs and arms and buttocks under the water and in and out.

The sumo swims from above dipping on the ocean tray.

The ripple of pinched buttocks not seen as its limbs rise from the blue barely move when on the surface.

The greyhound doe flies in the stagnant air of the wrestling arena empty with only the swaddled knees moving, the doe beside her, who's moving bound in the heavy robes. The blackened teeth surrounded by white powder open, as she gazes on the flicking doe.

Greyhound in that small space flies with its legs drawn up on it as if it is a fly caught beside the bound heavy robes. It flies by her and returns to her who's moving with swaddled knees on the rim of air hanging beneath it, the stream with the doe flicking above.

The robes are behind her.

Sumo is very gently coming to her on the rim.

A stain appears on her front spreading rose circle and she dies.

Appendix

The Sky of Text

The hump (Akira) floating on the waves of the night curled legless is identifiable in the fiery horizon, hanging visible in it.

It has no existence except its repetition.

The flying whorl ruffling in the night is a steel banded legless which comes to her and comes in her arms.

The analytical sense stymied having been violated come up and meet on that which is visible, the horizon line.

He floats in the black on his own ejaculated stream.

The analytical mind (of one's own, but apparently not in one) overriding and some inchoate principle which is felt are both empty paired. For this is only seen where seeing is not a medium for its expression.

They move, are only that, and are only existing when in relation to each other.

The suppressed is translated as an image. Yet the living world is suppressed, it is in fact. Akira is a man who in the text has been wounded and is out on the street where worm-like faceless figures in silk suits attack people. They're in L.A. in the setting of a sumo wrestling ring.

The analytical being flying in the ocean of the wide illumined blue fired air (is) suppressed and alone.—it is without direction but, from that, only appears to have direction.

(Akira had put the member in floating on that same night, but then carried by the worm man.

Had been stabbed by the same billowing figure worm flying when entering the wrestling ring, where a sumo had been stabbed, the entrails released in the dawn as the hippo I saw veering on the path met at dawn there the path is in the center of the bullrushes, only there. A light dawn, he's carried at night. Without mind which action is, at dawn with the worm flying hanging holds him. This is a continuance of the series. Arbitrarily, though not completely
the man vomits a dazzling blue, in the same night air.)

The former first lady trotting and then pulling with her muzzle her legs shaking trembling as she's dragging the wieners out of a woman on a field far away
runs to a cobalt cloud with the wieners. (out on the plain).
This contains no violence as it is empty and real.

The head of the pink tulip, bunches of them fully open are blind—and aren't born; are eyeless and not born, or are born and are in fields where one cow is blowing
it moves in the fields whether it's disturbing them; they're not born and are existing anyway, it moves in them.
They have this peaceful but wild existence—where everything's disturbed in it, but not by them
if the cow's behind it doesn't suffer and is observant, the tulips not being born (bourne) and being pink rushes

The Red Sea not to see filled with the violent pink rushes sustains the cow to have it wade, to have it walk.

One'd (only) rather be flattered and live in that fake circumstance than live in reality.
Others are treated like dogs as the means of flattering them.

This is to isolate the shape or empty interior of some events real in time so their 'arbitrary' location to each other emerges to, whatever they are.

To scrutinize their forms is to see the interior relation of experience.

He was not reincarnated as her because people did not know freedom.

Being completely free he had emerged in her.

This had occurred as her because her father had been wandering, young, before her birth, with a truck picking up those who surrendered?

One must not have any tradition in order to have been reincarnated.

Narrative 'solely' is the same as hanging within the 'visible' horizon *as being* its existence.

It narrows to and *is* the blue night.

The living world is suppressed really so the description of the action of landscape and time removes the action into the non-human.

The line of sky and earth is formed throughout the text by a forced will of one—by making the pearl sky and rose line—so that there is no other possibility except they're meeting.

The moon in a clearing surrounded by the puckering rivulets hangs and runs. It is above one, who is surrounded by the ocean of blind pink tulips.

The white waves (in a vast terraced puckering) of the night sky make an ocean of night, which doesn't reflect the ocean. The pink tulips that are not born are the ocean.

Where there's only color, the pink tulips not born, the (a) person still dies.

Red fireflies light stream. There's nothing to keep them down. There's no sleep existing. They don't wade. Cattle walk.

The red fireflies that float to the bottom line of the puckered night sky swim over the pink tulips that are blind. That isn't death.

The inchoate sense is a 'principle' in that it appears to have direction, yet this is illusion.
Visible is only repetition.

there is no visible sky on its own (in this nature).

The analytical empty meandering is at rest (not stilled). It jumps circuit
in great disturbance (it used to), created disturbance to make it jump circuit—a round which it creates.
since it is always paired (in one's nature), a conflict and quality of being alone which is its analytical circuit

(swimming over the earth looking down) (not as the romantic, modern, ego which is such by having no analytical component or other—or having such an other); but by reality (that's only present) being vivid in order to be real. It's alone to be visual.

Rather than taking the words from other texts, in places the text scrutinizes the apparent structures of these others, in the living world which is everywhere suppressed—(like a virus), makes the apparent structures here and there

where one eyes it quietly is now ruled by Bechtel—it only jumped circuit by creating its own disturbance in youth and involuntary in one, as the form of the early series.
It's like this wave coming to one when facing the actual outside ocean, it merely returns, in maturity, in one's own mind.

as the object of observation that is a half scene such as the moon lidded in the eyes of Akira (fictionalized) now wounded jetting on his own ejaculated stream over them.

They 'receive' no direct sight. We are not simply passive receptacles.

Bimbo steaming who had looking back pumped on a bicycle on a rise the golden thighs pinned to it motionless they're moving so heavily it doesn't move the air is in the thin blue.

One's the black butterfly at day, having dreamed at night. Dreamed seeing oneself asleep, aware of having to 'follow' or track the dream in it to have it be in the day, so tired that in the dream one wanted someone else to see the dream because one wanted to sleep in it, yet not being asleep in the day, that's it's being in the day,—being just the black butterfly there.

to waste someone

not being tired and (not) seeing oneself sleeping (though seeing) in the dream is it being in the day—?

The black butterfly in the thin blue is in the day

The analytical object of one's mind, without any pairs, any pairing, of clashing comparisons is brought within each other's range that have to exist only together.

Its repetition is vivid beauty, is not of anything else, is separate; and is to have simply that sky of dark blue and light blue also, but at night, 'exist' without sight producing or effecting it (the night) (which can't be produced by him).

Neither can be seen, where it's only that characteristic, of the visible, that's the focus, (as the black can't be in, or be seen in, the blue day, being night).

Akira had roiled there flew in the oil fires; one cow standing in the oil furnaces blew, in the livid pocked fires

There color is the only force.

gusts of tiny black birds
race and light in gusts—
his is the body that's died as existing

The silksuits who come up killing people at outdoor cafes at night are wicks—in the thin blue day.

They are equally paired, yet one or the other riding over-whelms the other
slip off and overwhelm it like the moon moving.
Here the actual events that are our conception of history normatively, what were, are real and are subject simply to being repeated in the landscape, and nowhere else implicitly. That's the only way in which it's history.
There in the series they're recycled, but exist only by being repeated, take on increasingly more beautiful shapes, the inner eye or soul of Bechtel, yet with our seeing that as it is.

If it's only conscious
If the fiction is the 'same' as the real events, where does it come from?
(If one's only conscious)

This is evolution which changes seeing.
so there is no other time (than action) or apprehension there.
we can't pay attention to anything slow increasingly.
Measure isn't even time but contentless apprehension.
Therefore the seeing of anything now has to be faster than prior sights, to increase action in order for it to be seen, to enter the attention, at all.
We learn and then use up the 'sight' cognitively, or use up the content, and thus quicken the apprehension.
So reading, focusing only on itself, can slow to be only apprehension
reading as apprehension *per se*, so it is slow
has no content but that
Motion is a thing in itself; it is a reality
qualitatively different than 'what it connects'
motion is apprehension, of its emptiness

aware of its emptiness
having no entity which apprehends
One could slow this so as
to see apprehension
scenes that have only that

scenes have entity for they
are volition

The buttocks of the men
moving in black—which can't be seen in the blue
is barely movement

The sack within doesn't breathe when it's still but one has
a clear light knowledge.
One vomits a dazzling blue.

Its own self chases in utter conflict
but opens; this is when one is awake

it's to be driven into being
a nomad.

It's seeing its structure only from within or as the inner
eye of Bechtel.
Yet the structure or oneself is in no way affected by this.
Akira is H.D.'s thousand-petalled lily

The hippo veering on the path at dawn pear-eyed isn't
born then

if I'm at this age at the state of being eighteen at dawn
(after the operation taking my neck out) where there's no death.
I have to reach that state, of being that at dawn.
There's no death possible at all, if one is eighteen again
not a child at dawn after, and with no pain.
The boat black butterfly isn't visible in day.

It didn't make any difference that it was day since it had no weight. Then, (seeing that?) night hadn't weight.

It has no weight, cattle walk in it.

even a feeling is the flutter of the neck taken out. the pinched butterfly is plowing in the water far off.

it isn't a live cornea, while it sees, or is only alive—trying to combine almost the inner shape of different cultures—as the interior of oneself falsely and intimately.

I was 'invaded' impinged upon by a dream which I couldn't remember and which was trying to enter into my waking state while I was standing there.

I want to get the outside real event to enter into the waking state in that way, to see it.

The compressions of the real into one's waking state streaming clearly in the midst of it form.

Where?—as if they have no future.

◦ٷ

Though the impinging dream in flickers had been frightening apparently, that may be its condition as being dream only. Not realizing (or realizing) that it is life.

The waking state in an ordinary lucid moment is the same as the dream.

Supposing one saw oneself as someone else, literally—in day. And one was

We have an impossible relation to life—in which there's no visual reflection. The head of the coconut vendor smashed by their soldiers, he lies dead in the street.

One walked through the frogs at night with the moon up and the roiling floating figure of a man jetting on his own curled hump that is on his ejaculated black stream in the black ahead;—in early traveling continually, so that there is only the approximation of intimacy 'here' having no place, the illusion itself as such in no place later is 'that' intimacy.

The fields of frogs making sounds on the moonlit wet rungs stretching before one, the black night is filled with stars. Hardly visible the black floating hump of the man hangs separate ahead of one. This is a continuation where there are only inner actions, not changing their forms.

Their military having deposed the people's elected leader —we're to return him

ours makes an agreement with theirs to oust themselves— who were killing people in cafes at day—and soldiers landing there watch them kill people in the street, doing nothing— saying we're only to maintain government order, so it is theirs.

Dreams come from day? The physical visual reflections of figures to each other are as the same—have no features—as in a dream or day. So one is only at day.

People reflect each other visually as if they are the same entities—at day, rather than their being dreams.

Our bureaucrats about their, whom we're to oust, clubbing the people to death in front of the passive soldiers, ours who've poured in—say theirs are trained in those actions, that clubbing is their response *per se*. When they respond it's that. Oh.

I can't rest. One's mind is the inside movements of the events, that are outside—it is literally the outside; beating the bushes so it would have no other place to go.

The cobalt sky is light blue, though it is night. White clouds are in the empty cobalt sky as men trumpeting slide in the crowd which is playing ball. A crowd is eating, walking.

I don't think anything meets in the thin cobalt. Maybe the cigarette fume is the same thing as it. Cloud drifts in it.

Curled figure-bow as the leg is pinned like a sling-shot is a beggar lying in the doorway.

It's like flying in the blue.

The night causes rest—eventually, itself causing. As that appears one notices it.

In day the blue of the sky having invaded the ground of city—where the blue cannot be reflected—it isn't reflected and isn't itself water there.

In the dim glare of the vast lawn surrounded by monumental slabs men with almost shaved razor heads play ball. They kick up a ball, running with or after it. Slim and almost nude, they look the same, in the heat playing ball—with the shaved razor heads, in the capital, as being.

The one is not paired with the other.

The day is like this without any pair.

reading is sole

Pairs do not occur, in that a movement occurs first by itself.

At night the dim lighted folds hang vastly, lights on cycles hundreds of them ride forward.

People crossing the cars and scooters with beams head-on the night with its folds hangs in immense folds.

Their not skinheads yet almost a V on the shaved razor heads of the slight almost nude men playing ball on the dim glare of green.

In a garden of other flowering trees, looking through a stone grill, one hears a bird with a radical trill which drops losing everything and repeats and repeats. That one bird is to return as joy where it drops losing everything there and repeats.

A comparison of two cultures is in what is seen in the physical world and what occurs in the same physical world.

Immense bands in the faint blue sky, that don't drift, the sky has buildings in it and racing cars amidst the sheet of cycles.

The sheet of cycles descends though on a flat plain in the

cloud bands, immense bar, existing in the sky—not existing in hierarchy. The sheet is even in the vaulted horizonless plain.

as the characteristic of paradise

as events *per se*

As continual change is the sole ideal, adventure is the sole ideal—yet it is not neutral rather as existence *per se.*

The bow of the curled sprung dying person is even with adventure.

Hovering in paradise so that there is nowhere to go in continual change is given up. There may be nowhere to go and no paradise—and no interiority in which to go.

The person, the black butterfly, can't enter as there's no paradise—and there's no inner being—except as nonbeing. That isn't choosing to be an ordinary being, because it is.

The shaved razor heads playing ball almost nude on the sweltering dim green seen as fashion are rather soldiers with the same body, with no fat, in the capital as being.

Seated on a bench on the green watching the shaved razor heads playing ball far off, in the capital, one deciphers this real movement from that of dreaming, while asleep or not, any-where, and the real action being the same as dreamed.

This is traveling continually yet having no interiority in which to go.

The warm embrace of the man who now jetting on his own ejaculated stream—the indigo not even folds.

One can't even look in or outward in the folds, in an action, and as ordinary being. Neither he nor the night, as one—are inner, are oneself.

The almost nude men, with the same body, in the capital, some walking by or playing ball, on the sweltering green, dim, is continual travel which—spring, the neck cut out—is just out there, not hierarchical

as long as the events observing

only—occur

They occur without imposition. One doesn't 'learn' anything—spring, the neck cut out—is inner, where there isn't any.

If there is no relation of actual events to writing—caught in the military in the World War in the encircling events, a vast terrain fighting in assigned suicides; starving; thirty millions died, as if life were nothing to anyone—there is only adventure outside in life (a pair), (as events are not writing). This is free it's unrelated to writing—so there's only adventure.

The terrifying is in realizing that the event is life—then traveling is unnecessary and calm.

That something having been dreamed, which I didn't remember, would enter the entirely waking state and assert itself, unremembered, forcing flickers of itself into the conscious moment—is a pair, in which life is sole.

᠁

this is 'history' as being in 'its' present time, seen from within as if present time's reverse side, where aftermath from this is illusion.

that as the place whose conception is that of not having authority so that one in bowing is doing so to that.

if one doesn't have authority, one won't bow
without authority, and one bows
not having any is bowing
The figure's bowing as the fiery dark trees unfurling are in the light blue

In the Red Sea, water's red
sun
looking at the oily blue

bowing's being a bat
at dusk no looking
a person's being blind, where
the place is only visible
the sun's not born; that
doesn't mirror the Red Sea
the oily blue's bat, as flying on it,
it doesn't produce it, so one's
close to (anyone's) death
an instant sun (rolls).

everyone's young flowers and then dead which doesn't
exist really, as it is an instant, is easy

The men and women who are bimbos on boards sink in
the green wave.
They go down standing in the wave.
Curling on the wave, yet of night, the dark hump figure
banded floating to her comes in her arms.

One has to have a different job each time so as not to
learn, the connecting links being removed. There one has to
learn something once.

One sees the physical body, theirs, has no end.
dog's yap on the oily blue
transacted by air
incinerated worm
(yet it's night instantly) finning
on its yolk

oar of the oily blue a single
oar

In the morning, there's no oar. A blind woman on the
sea, the boat floating, a bat on the red water isn't at dusk, can't
be or exist at dusk.

I saw almost-yellow almost-nude shaved, nude heads as of monks, men lying with only their imprints around them on walls, except for each other. It's like they're yellow butterflies entering the air, they're not moving, that is not black or blue so it is devoid of it, devoid of any black or any blue air there.

(Sankai Juku. 'we're' seeing 'culture' having occurrence inside only)

In the light elation where there is no end to physical existence for anyone, a worry is only fostered, before coming up to and meeting any circumstance even doesn't exist.

The struggle one feels to ready oneself to be in any circumstance—in blossoming trees—or to form a resistance, has no occurrence even.

History is hearing the minute throughout the series (of events), with no sound structure imposed on them. They *could* have a sound structure imposed on them and be utterly free also.

only occurrence *per se*
darkens intellect here

Events here become the inside of *this*, by being its fiction.

Jena Osman's *Amblyopia* continually makes the periphery, as if that were the edge of the object, at which something/oneself is seen. The faculty of perception is itself time, as the shape in/of the writing; and in that sense it is an object observing itself. Osman says an action can't be remembered that is out of control; yet the coherence which is 'given' experience, or lack of coherence, is lighted or observed 'from the inside': "What is inside after having stayed inside for this length. Light brings memory out from the inside."

In this being analysis of another poet's writing, it's *imitating* analysis of theirs here. *They're* utterly free.

Only Defoe is myself as when I'm in utter ignorance.

If sight creates thinking—corresponding locations, cognition, being created in the brain from the sights—sound creates phenomena throughout places (even sleep)

a sound creates duration of phenomena

The heavy back rising and falling, on the open sea, lace falls off of it when it's risen.

It submerged again, lace closing.

The ocean makes a hollow sound when the sumo slaps it, rising and falling forward as he swims.

The dogs crowd forward seizing a figure on a ghat. People are helpless in life.

Crowds are in a dirge for a man who having been ill is dying.

The crowd in the dusk crying has only empty retinas.

In the blazing blue they cry for infants.

There's an inflamation, an iris, between them

Amerigo Vespucci couples a deer. Collaboration is calm.

The flickering tongue of the blind woman on the visible Red Sea, the water's red, is in the visual reality—for her.

The flaps of the iris are in her within blind flicking her tongue outside.

Some are naked as in being ferried on Lethé and an iris is between them here and there now in the water.

UNIVERSITY PRESS OF NEW ENGLAND

publishes book under its own imprint and is the publisher for Bran-
deis University Press, Dartmouth College, Middlebury College Press,
University of New Hampshire, University of Rhode Island, Tufts
University, University of Vermont, Wesleyan University Press, and
Salzburg Seminar.

ABOUT THE AUTHOR

Leslie Scalapino is the author of numerous books of poetry, essays,
and plays, as well as the novel *Defoe* (Sun & Moon, 1994). Among
her books of poetry are *way* (1988), *that they were at the beach—
aeolotropic series* (1985), and *Considering how exaggerated music is*
(1982), all published by North Point Press.

LIBRARY OF CONGRESS CATALOGING-IN-PUBLICATION DATA

Scalapino, Leslie, 1947–

The front matter, dead souls / Leslie Scalapino.

p.   cm. (Wesleyan Poetry)

ISBN 0–8195–5290–9 (cloth : alk. paper). — ISBN 0–8195–6295–5

(pbk. : alk. paper)

I. Title.

PS3569.C253F76   1996

813'.54—dc20   95–35718